The Return of the Martians

A sequel to "The War of the Worlds"

Mark Hood

UNSEELIE PRESS

Unseelie Press

Cover design by MiblArt
miblart.com

Get your free book!

Visit my website to claim your free book, "Amy's Journal".

https://ares.watch/amy

During the first Martian invasion, we all know what happened to our narrator. But after he left his wife in the care of her cousin in Leatherhead, what happened to her?

Abandoned by her husband amidst the terror of the Martian Invasion, Amy battles to help those in need and save lives. But when the war arrives on her doorstep, can she save herself?

For Martyne, as always.

Contents

Chapter One

Woking

The nightmares became more frequent as Mars moved into opposition. My terror regularly awoke my wife, and she in turn roused me from dreams in which I found myself buried alive, or forced to murder my fellow men to ensure my escape from terrors lurking in the shadows.

I knew well what those unseen threats represented. Two years had passed since the terrible events of the Martian invasion, and those creatures still haunted my dreams.

"Will you write today?" Amy asked, almost casually, over our morning toast. I grunted in reply, unwilling to commit to a proper answer. "You have written nothing in some time, and I know your publisher wrote to you yesterday. How is it coming along?"

"It isn't, as you well know," I snapped, and instantly regretted it. A pause extended painfully as she poured me another cup of tea. "I simply cannot concentrate at present. We're not ready for when they come back. And against that knowledge, it is hard to summon any reason to write."

"It's also hard to summon the next month's rent," she said, shaking the empty biscuit tin. "If the words for the book will not come, perhaps another article? You had that idea about a retrospective on the time since the... incidents, and what we as a society had learned. Perhaps it's time to work on that?"

I chewed my toast as I considered her idea, watching the squirrels in the garden gathering nuts against the coming winter. "But we've learned dashed little, as far as I can see." It is remarkable how quickly men's minds turned back to mundane matters. Within a few months after the death of the Martian invaders, barely a man on the street showed any signs of concern at the possibility of their return.

I would be remiss if I gave the impression that all men were unperturbed — those of us who saw the Martians first-hand or lost loved ones to their attacks are all too aware of the danger the red planet holds. And there are some who expect them to return any day now, and agitate for more defences, myself among them.

"Perhaps another letter to the *Times*," I mused.

Amy's voice echoed from the pantry. "They didn't see fit to print your last three." A clattering and banging erupted from the small room, and at the sound of her cry of pain, I leapt to her aid. I found her sat upon the floor, tins of peaches scattered around her. "This dashed stockpile of yours," she grumbled, "will be the death of me." I helped her up and began to re-stack the tins more carefully.

"You'll be glad of it when the Martians return," I reminded her.

Amy scoffed and rubbed the blossoming bruise on her elbow. "To hell with the Martians, and the Devil take your tinned goods. It's not enough I lose my rose-bushes to a vegetable plot, but now you risk our home over this obsession?"

"To do nothing is the greater risk, and that is all I see happening around me. We lie unprepared, unguarded and defenceless."

"What little faith you have. Do you not trust the government to have its citizen's best interests at heart? Recall the replies to your letters, when the *Times* still printed them. 'Every measure' is being explored, they said."

"And yet they present no evidence of their preparations," I protested. "The man in the street does not know what to do when the invasion comes, and indeed they are all but encouraged not to think of it." The machine that once towered over Primrose Hill has gone for scrap, the Martian kept preserved under spirits in the Natural History Museum is consigned to a basement and so the last visible reminders of our peril are gone from our sight. I often wonder whether they did this for economic reasons, or because such a reminder of our inferiority was embarrassing for those in charge. There are even those who no longer truly believe the event occurred — outside the areas of Surrey and London where the fighting machines strode, the tale has frequently been viewed as exaggeration if not outright fabrication.

Amy left the pantry and returned to the breakfast table. "They do not wish to spread panic unnecessarily. But if you truly believe nothing is being done, then why not visit Frederick in London? You told me he was involved in our preparations for any potential return. Perhaps speaking with him again will help ease your mind? When you see how things are being planned for, it might allow you to turn your mind away from it all."

It is true that my brother had become involved in our contingency planning. He had been a junior administrator before the first invasion, but earned promotion by virtue of his experiences during that time and his acumen for planning. In fact, he had been so busy during the first months in his new position that we had quite fallen out of touch, my letters going unanswered except for the occasional telegram informing me he was quite well and extremely busy. How long had it been since we last spoke face to face? Almost a year, I fancied.

"He'll be too busy to see me," I said.

"Which is it, that the Government does nothing or that they are rushed off their feet? I am sure he will make time for a luncheon with his brother, even without an appointment. Go, it will do you good to be out of the house for a while. Just promise me you won't abandon your writing for a new life in government planning, should he ask you."

As we bickered, we did not know that my worst fears would soon come to fruition.

———◄O►———

Aboard the train to London, I reminisced about my own efforts to spread awareness. While the threat remained, I had felt duty-bound to keep the issue foremost in the minds of my fellow man. Regardless of any confidence in the Government's preparations, it would be for nothing if the man or woman in the street did not take the situation seriously. I had therefore taken responsibility upon myself.

With the *Times* no longer feeling the need to print my letters, and not being of the disposition to take to shouting from street corners, my options for disseminating my opinions were limited. I had resolved to take my message to places where I had hope of it being heeded, and had booked a series of speaking engagements at town halls and working men's clubs across the Surrey area. As far as the venues were aware, I planned to discuss my book and my experiences depicted therein, but my goal was to spread a warning of the Martian's imminent return and to encourage suitable preparations to be made among the populace.

I had started on my back doorstep, in a manner of speaking.

My first experiment had been in the saloon bar of the Spotted Dog. This was well renowned as a place of lively discourse, though conversation was more often than not limited to the prices of livestock at the marketplaces and auction houses across the county. However, as a regular visitor, they gave me the benefit of the doubt when I proposed a discussion one warm Friday evening the previous summer.

"Gentlemen," I began. "I believe I am known to most of you by reputation, if not personally. And at the risk of appearing a caricature of myself, I do indeed wish to talk about the Martians again." A chorus of good natured cheers, groans and the odd cry of "Off!" greeted this pronouncement, but I pressed on. "There is a good chance of their return, and we must prepare for that eventuality. The Government assures me that even now they are taking steps to ensure your safety, but I must urge you all to do your part as well."

"I'll 'appily sneeze on any Mars-man who comes near me," one wag called out, to general laughter.

I smiled; if I was to win over this crowd, and perhaps a wider one, I needed not to lambast them. "And we all thank you for that," I replied, to another round of chuckles. "But I speak more of preparation. I believe we should each lay in some small supplies to protect against shortages and interruptions to deliveries. And contrive a plan for what each of us might do in the event of a Martian landing nearby again." I saw looks of consternation cross a few of the faces before me, I was truly being heeded. "Perhaps you would stay and fight, perhaps leave to seek safety elsewhere. Whatever your goal, think on it now and then be ready to put it in motion when the time comes."

"If, if the time comes," a quiet voice called out. I nodded assent.

"Indeed, none of this is certainty. But it will do you no harm to behave as if it were. Forewarned is forearmed, after all."

Silence greeted my words.

Of all the outcomes I had expected, this was not one. While I had never dared to imagine full-throated assent to my suggestions, I had hoped that I might have swayed opinion because of my prior experience. I had prepared for dissent, of course, for arguments against taking up arms and inviting retribution by the invaders, but never had I imagined utter disinterest as a response.

A gentle cough broke through the awkward hush. As one, my audience turned to the party responsible, who withered under the sudden attention.

"Did you wish to say something?" I asked.

A small man in well-worn overalls stood up awkwardly. I vaguely recognised him as a worker on one of the nearby farms. "Well, the thing is, sir," he mumbled, "why's it got to be us?" A murmur of agreement went through the crowd at this, which emboldened him. "We've 'ad our turn, as I see it, we 'ad 'em right on our doorsteps, so it's someone else's go, if you ask me." A chorus of "hear, hear" filled the smoky room.

"It's every man's fight," I began, but was soon drowned out by other voices.

"Joe's right," one said, naming the small man. "We've done our bit. Let some other buggers have a crack at 'em." This was met with cheers. Now the floodgates were opened, the true feelings of this group were made clear. Even if the Martians were to return, Woking had seen and done enough. I suspected that beneath this selfish notion lay a deeper truth, that considering the possibility of the invader's return was too terrifying to give thought to, and so any erstwhile excuse was seized upon as a reason to avoid it.

I retreated from the pub as soon as I could and licked my wounds. Despite my wife's urging, I continued with my planned talks, though I scarcely found a better reception at any. Similar reasoning was put forward at those locations which had seen Martians during the previous invasion, that it was time for someone else to take charge. Only among the few towns I visited which had escaped attention did anyone appear to take my advice seriously, but even then they were loath to do anything about it. Once again, the notion of the return of the fighting machines was thought simultaneously too frightening and so unlikely as to not bear any serious thought. Most people believed the Martians would not dare to return, while the rest remained confident that we would stop them long before they left their cylinders.

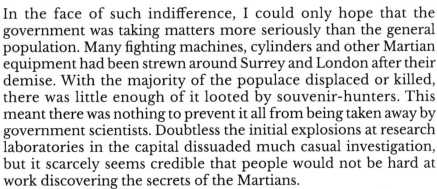

In the face of such indifference, I could only hope that the government was taking matters more seriously than the general population. Many fighting machines, cylinders and other Martian equipment had been strewn around Surrey and London after their demise. With the majority of the populace displaced or killed, there was little enough of it looted by souvenir-hunters. This meant there was nothing to prevent it all from being taken away by government scientists. Doubtless the initial explosions at research laboratories in the capital dissuaded much casual investigation, but it scarcely seems credible that people would not be hard at work discovering the secrets of the Martians.

Indeed, some dramatic developments in technology can be attributed to the legacy of the invasion. Telegraphs are more efficient, bringing news from around the world. Wireless broadcasts have greater range and quality than ever before, and even distant parts of the Empire are now more easily reached and governed. There are even plans for a device that will bring images into people's homes in the same way as radio brings distant voices to us.

Whether any of those secrets are being shared with the world at large, however, is unlikely. Where an opportunity for profit existed, patents were filed to ensure that only British companies would reap the benefits. Any developments with a military or defensive application were immediately classified, and any work continued in secret. The politicians, of course, have the good of the nation to consider, and would not want to arm any past or future adversary.

But those of us with a wider view believe that Europe- or World-wide preparations shall be required to face down a second, more concerted threat. For that to happen, cooperation is vital. We must share what we have learned about the Martian weaknesses, and our allies around the world should be involved in the defensive planning.

One of my friends is a member of the London Club frequented by many of the political classes, and reports that this view is not shared by many in Government. The more short-sighted of the Cabinet have prevailed over their colleagues, and convinced them we must squirrel away our prizes and any discoveries made from them in the hopes of an advantage over any future adversary. Among this group, they make much of the Indian Rebellion and the war in Crimea as precursors to another, global conflict to come. Those who fear that the war will be against Mars, and argue that humanity must unite and pull together, are ridiculed. A comic in *Punch* satirised this view, picturing the Prime Minister looking into a microscope and asking an aide "But how can I shake hands with our new allies?" When the tiniest creatures in a drop of water can fell your enemy, why bother working with our human neighbours?

Such confidence was exposed as merely superficial that morning, and I witnessed the beginning of mankind's descent with sadness more than fear.

Chapter Two

Brother

U pon arriving in London, I strolled along to Whitehall. Around me the once-ruined buildings had mostly been rebuilt, new and clean against the soot-blackened exteriors of their neighbours. Scaffolding obscured the facade of the building in which my brother worked, where tradesmen were busy repairing the gargoyles and bas-reliefs. Even hidden away, it formed an imposing edifice, with busy men in suits coming and going at pace from its oversized front doors. I watched with a shudder one of the handling cranes lifting vast blocks of stone with the long, tentacle-like manipulators we had developed from the Martian's machinery.

Inside, I found a woman working at the front desk who promised to have a message taken to Frederick. I informed him via this means that I intended to be at the Silver Cross Inn at one o'clock, and would be happy to buy him his luncheon.

With time to kill until that hour, and the early autumn air crisp and inviting, I sauntered over to Hyde Park. Around the area were more open lots, small piles of rubble testifying to the previous existence of buildings on the site. The long grass and robust weeds signalled it had been some time since anyone had visited. I wondered at the residents of these once-glorious homes. Had they fled London ahead of the black smoke, or perished in their residences, hoping the threat would pass them by?

I heard a jeering crowd over at Speaker's Corner and hurried over. I had to push through a few rows of curious onlookers before I could make out what the speaker had to say over the catcalls and boos from his audience.

"Repent, repent, brothers, or He shall cleanse us from the Earth. If we do not show ourselves worthy of this world, He shall offer it to another!"

An image of the poor curate sprang unbidden to my mind, his lifeless eyes staring at me. The world contracted around me, tunnels narrowing my vision until all I could see was the man atop his soap box. As swiftly as it had arrived, the panic left me.

The speaker was one of the 'fire and brimstone' preachers so common these days, but this alone would not be enough to justify his treatment. As he continued in his sermon, however, I understood why he had stirred such powerful emotions.

"That last visitation was a warning, and will be our last! We have not heeded His words, and so he will dispatch His chosen ones to replace us all!"

The surrounding dissent grew louder, and when someone hurled missiles at the speaker, he turned tail and ran amidst much jeering. The crowd congratulated themselves on seeing off a dangerous heretic and dispersed.

I wish I could report that this was the first such preacher I had encountered, but in fact, they had become quite common since the coming of the Martians. The curate would no doubt have been among their number. This group views the invaders either as The Flood, ready to wipe mankind from the face of the Earth; The Chosen who will inherit the planet when we are gone, or The Devil who will punish us for eternity for our sins, or some combination thereof. This gentleman appeared to be a member of one or both of the first two camps.

The majority opinion in the country was that all of these views were wrong. The public knows that the Martians lost the war, even if they do not understand the details, and believe that they will not trouble us again. Among this group, the prevailing view was that the Martians will choose to occupy Venus instead, an opinion given weight by the astronomical observations by Lessing of markings on that planet's disc. Though it would be inappropriate of me to suggest that such matters even merited discussion by most — the subject of Martians rarely came up for discussion, and once the first few weeks had passed after the invasion, any attempt to broach the topic had met with indifference or hostility at 'opening up old wounds'.

The crowd appeared more concerned with the behaviour of the trouble maker than any imminent danger they themselves might be under. I approached one to ask why he had taken such an issue with the preacher.

"They're not coming here," he said, with all the confidence he could muster. "They're off somewhere else. We gave them such a drubbing they'd never dare show their ugly faces around here again."

I wished I could share his conviction.

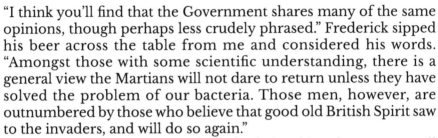

"I think you'll find that the Government shares many of the same opinions, though perhaps less crudely phrased." Frederick sipped his beer across the table from me and considered his words. "Amongst those with some scientific understanding, there is a general view the Martians will not dare to return unless they have solved the problem of our bacteria. Those men, however, are outnumbered by those who believe that good old British Spirit saw to the invaders, and will do so again."

"It is as I feared," I muttered. "Nobody is taking the matter at all seriously."

"Many of us are," he said. He paused while a waitress delivered our beef Wellington. "That's what's been keeping me so busy of late, organising our activities and arranging funding. It is a constant battle against those who view every shilling spent on our preparations as money wasted, especially considering the tensions in Europe."

"Tensions they themselves contributed to," I interjected, "by refusing to share the Martian technology we captured or salvaged."

He smiled. "True enough, although things were bound to come to a head, eventually. The race to arms was inevitable. As technology improved, our perceived superiority merely accelerated matters. And once it began, there was even less of an appetite for sharing the details."

"But wouldn't the prospect of a war on the continent focus the Government's attention on learning the most from the Martians? Their weapons could give us a decisive advantage should hostilities break out."

"If we could get them working," he shrugged. "Their power sources are a mystery, and when the early experiments with the heat-ray backfired, the War Office quite lost its appetite for the subject. Such research as continues now is scientific, rather than military."

My beef threatened to stick in my dry throat. "So are we defenceless?" I asked. "When they return..."

"If," my brother corrected me. "It's not yet certain they will do so, or choose to come here." His voice carried, as if he wanted his words to be heard. I waved my hand to dismiss his interruption.

"When. Are we to just stand by as they march through London, send their black smoke up this street again?" I heard my voice cracking and noticed people at nearby tables looking over at us.

There was a lengthy pause as Frederick mulled something over in his mind. Eventually, he leaned closer to me across the sticky table and spoke in low tones.

"There are others who believe as you do, and are working on a response should that scenario occur. Our activities are not official, but nor are they entirely 'off the books' either. I have obscured some of the more outlandish requests among dry technical reports and budget procurements, which go unread by our Lords and Masters. Perhaps a meeting will help ease your mind somewhat?" He leaned back and continued eating. "How is Amy, by the way? I trust she is well?"

His mention of my wife brought to mind her words that morning, and the use of the phrase 'ease your mind' by both. I had to assume his enquiry after her was merely politeness and an attempt to change the subject, nothing more. His use of the same words had to be coincidental. If he had no time to write to me, then he would not have communicated with her either.

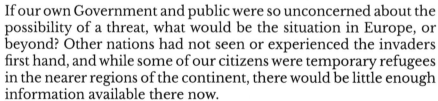

If our own Government and public were so unconcerned about the possibility of a threat, what would be the situation in Europe, or beyond? Other nations had not seen or experienced the invaders first hand, and while some of our citizens were temporary refugees in the nearer regions of the continent, there would be little enough information available there now.

As one who has gathered a modicum of renown because of my account of the invasion, I have occasionally spoken at gatherings of the learned. There at least I found those few who have concern at what was coming. They believed as I did that a return was inevitable — the Martians could not ignore the comfort and resources offered by our world while their own lies dying, and they will have learned from their mistakes. No stroke of luck and friendly bacteria will save us this time.

Even among men in such agreement there is room for discussion — in fact, I feel that the meetings are only a front for a debating society. At the gathering in August, Mr Watt-Evans cornered me and expounded on his pet theories for some time. He believes the invasion was in fact nothing of the sort, a point of view he shares with anyone who will listen, or at least who does not actively avoid him.

"If they had truly intended to conquer us, then they were far too few — a mere ten cylinders against the entire planet?"

"A scouting party, then," I protested.

"They had no means of return to their home, so they would have been very poor scouts. And they equipped themselves extraordinarily badly; by your own account, they had not even thought to bring a ladder to leave their cylinder, but fell instead to the ground!"

"They did well enough, despite that," I reminded him with a shudder. "That heat-ray alone could have wiped us all out."

"But they didn't wish to wipe us out, they needed us for food. And the nation would have risen against them, in time, and overwhelmed them. No, I do not believe they wished to be here at all."

Imagine the Martian situation — a dying planet, canals dug to bring what little water remained to the vast cities. Those cities all but empty as civilisation teeters on the brink of annihilation. And picture the dissent among the population, the exasperation at a Government unable to provide for its people (or whatever those creatures called themselves). It is not a great mental leap to imagine some Martian equivalent of the Chartists fomenting protests, strikes and riots to improve their lot.

Faced with such an insurrection, what would the leaders do? In our own history, the leaders of such rebellions were transported, the death penalty being seen as too severe a punishment and perhaps the same is true of Mars. Watt-Evans' own view is that this was the source of our 'invaders' — that they were exiles. Perhaps they were soldiers who had attempted a coup against their Martian rulers and were sent to die on a hostile Earth as punishment. Or perhaps violent protesters, trade unionists, or other group the Martian leaders felt undesirable.

The non-falsifiable nature of his theory does him little credit as a man of science, and it is not widely accepted. It makes little difference — if we are to be a prison colony for these creatures, then we should still prepare for another shipment of convicts.

After our repast, and the customary good-natured dispute over who ought to pay the bill, we returned to my brother's offices.

Frederick spoke to the woman at the reception desk and enquired after one of his colleagues.

"Chambers? Yes, he is in at present, although he left instructions he doesn't wish to be disturbed."

"Oh, he won't mind me. Nor my brother, I know he will want to meet him. You can always tell him you tried valiantly to stop me but that I outpaced you across the lobby." He smiled at her, and once again I noticed the effect his effortless charm had upon the members of the opposite sex as the woman stifled a smile and turned aside to hide her blushing. "Come along," he called to me, and set off across the marble floor towards the staircase.

Rather than ascending to a higher floor, as I had expected, he led me down into the basement of the building. The walls were unfinished, the floor rough compared to the fine stone slabs we had recently seen. A scent of damp pervaded the place, and I struggled to imagine who could enjoy working in such a place. We arrived at a plain wooden door, warped such that the top corner allowed a glimmer of green light to escape between door and frame. Someone had pinned a notice to the door with brass drawing pins, now tarnished and staining the paper green. The sign read 'Project Ares', written in large, neat letters. Below in a different hand was a note presumably added later which read 'Little green men keep out!' beside a crude drawing of a tripod.

Frederick knocked and opened the door without waiting for an invitation to enter. Green light spilled out around him and momentarily blinded me. Squinting against the brightness, I followed him inside.

Chapter Three

Chambers

"I said not to disturb me!" a voice called from inside. "Oh, it's you..." he tailed off as he recognised my brother.

My eyes slowly adjusted to the brightness, and I looked around in wonder. My attention was first drawn to the rear of this space, where one of the Martian's fighting machines was stripped bare. It was the first one that I had seen in over a year, and still it sent shivers down my spine, even in its dismantled state. Wires ran into and out of the carapace, and several instruments were attached to it. The contraption's limbs and handling tentacles were removed, but the stumps twitched in apparent memory of striding the miles between Surrey and London. On the benches between myself and this dissection were other unfamiliar devices, presumably stripped from the shell for closer examination. One held what looked like a box camera, but in place of the lens apparatus an organic-looking eyeball twitched and moved uncannily. A glass-fronted box on the bench beside it showed a grainy moving image — with a start I realised it was a likeness of myself and I leaned closer. The blurred image moved in sympathy with me, my features swimming into focus. I regarded my surprised expression as it appeared on the screen and understood that this eye was providing the source of the image. Was this the means by which the Martian in his fighting machine surveyed the field of battle?

"It can display the image at practically any distance from the source," our host said with some pride. "At present the necessity of wires limits it, but we believe it can be transferred by radio."

"So you have been learning their secrets?" I asked.

"Some of them have yielded to our investigations," the man replied. "Some are still beyond us, but we can harness a few for our own ends."

My brother made the introductions, and I shook hands with Chambers, my eyes still roaming the basement workshop.

"The author of the popular account?" he asked when he heard my name. I nodded. "Oh, how wonderful, your brother has often mentioned you, but I didn't think I'd find the chance to meet with you. Hold on a moment," he said, and turned to rummage through the drawers of the desk at which he had been sitting. I regarded him curiously.

I wasn't sure what I had expected our lead investigator and erstwhile defender to look like, but I doubt I'd have imagined the slight figure before me now. His tweed suit was well worn, suede patches on the elbows in need of repair and the seams fraying around the lower edges of the jacket. His hair was similarly unkempt, his tie loose and askew, and his shoes had clearly not seen polish in some time. All in all, he gave me the impression of a man who spent more time inside his own head with his thoughts than interacting with other people.

"Ah ha!" he cried and brandished a dog-eared booklet. With a sinking heart, I realised it was a copy of my account of the first invasion. "Would you mind?" he asked, handing it to me along with a leaking fountain pen. I took it and signed my name on the title page for him, and he beamed as he took it back. "Thank you, most kind." He looked bashful for a moment. "Your work has been extremely valuable in my preparations, you know, I wish I could have been there, but your words almost transport me..." he stopped babbling as he regarded the look upon my face. "Of — of course, it must have been terrible," he stammered. "I meant merely that you describe the events so plainly one can imagine oneself there."

Frederick coughed gently, and then spoke. "Chambers, my brother has come here to see that we are not taking the Martian threat lightly."

Chambers nodded eagerly, his eyes lighting up. "Absolutely, I've been working on their technology around the clock. Fascinating stuff it is, too."

I stared at my brother incredulously. This one man was our response? This is how he proposed to assuage my fears of a lack of preparation? He clearly saw my consternation.

"Chambers here is our chief scientist, but we have other teams around the country putting his discoveries to work. Naturally keeping too many men at work in the capital would draw attention to our activities."

"I should like to show you something," Chambers urged, beckoning me to a table against the wall. With a glance over my shoulder at my brother's smiling face, I followed.

I had believed that the remote-viewing apparatus would have been the most advanced development I saw, but now I watched Chambers manipulating controls on a panel in front of him while on a neighbouring desk a miniature gun swivelled back and forth under his command. No wires connected the two.

"It works by radio," Chambers confirmed. "We hope to allow for unmanned artillery pieces before too long, which will reduce the loss of life should the Martians survive a first bombardment. Oh, and there's this of course."

We next inspected the dismantled fighting machine at the rear of the room, which had first attracted my attention. I could make no sense of the devices connected up to it, nor did Chambers' explanations illuminate me further, but what I understood was that they had deciphered the locomotive power behind the tripods. The Martians' principal source of energy came from the controlled decomposition of certain minerals, chiefly Uranium, and the research of Becquerel, Rutherford and others had been vital in understanding this. I seized upon the importance of international collaboration and attempted to sound out my guide's opinions on the matter.

"Our hands are tied," he sighed. "Government policy," — his words dripped with venom — "is that this work is all for Britain, and not to be shared with our usual research allies. Frankly, it limits our effectiveness — the application of various viewpoints and expertise is hugely beneficial in science, as it is in most fields."

Frederick intervened to head off Chambers' opinions on the inefficiency and obstinance of government, and suggested tea. Chambers busied himself with a small paraffin stove and a thin metal saucepan, still talking to me the whole time.

"You are one of the few who saw the Martians for any period and lived, and your account of the events of the invasion has been very helpful in our planning. We believe you have a great deal to offer us as we prepare."

I swallowed hard. "You flatter me, but I have set forth everything I observed in my writing. I do not know that I have anything else to impart."

"Your letters to the *Times* prove you have humanity's best interests in mind and are aware of the risk we face. We need a man of your talents and experience. So what say you, will you help us in our mission?"

Understand that I was reluctant to revisit those days again. That while I was content to debate the Martian threat and agitate for it to be taken seriously, I had no desire to involve myself, being happy for the authorities to address the issue. The sight of that carapace laid open had revived memories of the last days of the invasion, the crows pecking at the flesh that hung from the open machines. I fought down a shudder and tried to think rationally.

I had seen a measure of the preparations being made, the attempts to determine the secrets the Martian equipment held, and this at least gave me some small comfort. But one man in a mouldy basement, and who knows how few scattered around the country, could never be enough against an invasion. Would I be better to return to Woking, embrace my wife and trust in the government that all would be well?

I knew I could not do that. While the risk remained I owed it to her to ensure she would be safe. I had believed her lost once before and could not face that again.

I screwed up all my courage. "If there is some way in which I can aid you, I will," I stated. "You have my typewriter at your disposal, and I will endeavour to raise the need for collaboration and cooperation in the public's mind."

The relief Chambers felt showed on his face. "Thank you," he said. "My superiors are already bored with my complaints, but someone with first-hand knowledge and understanding will be harder to ignore.

"But there is one more thing we would request. It also relies on your prior experience, but could be of even greater importance to our work."

"I do not see how I have anything additional to offer."

"Drink your tea, and I will show you," Chambers smiled.

———◆○◆———

The tea was over-steeped and too bitter to drink, and my curiosity at what Chambers believed I could do to assist made me impatient. He eventually finished his tea with a satisfied sigh and led me out of the room.

Next door was a dingy space, much smaller than the first, with peeling wallpaper and black mould spreading across the ceiling.

I shuddered at its resemblance to the red weeds that had briefly overtaken our natural flora.

In the centre of the room, occupying almost all the available space, stood a giant oaken table that must have been a valuable antique before water damage claimed the lower portion of its legs. Upon it lay a relief map, hills and valleys represented by papier mâché mounds, and blue-painted streams. I recognised the areas around my home in Woking.

Scattered over the map were miniature figures of men, artillery guns, representations of the Martians' fighting machines and some other devices I did not recognise. Squat, boxy forms with multiple wheels and a gun-barrel projecting from the front stood in short ranks around the tripod.

Hanging from the walls were long wooden rods, presumably to move and position the figures, and chalkboards with tallies of losses and fatalities. I recognised the setup immediately — the boys in our village played a version of this on kitchen tables and parlour floors. In place of the youths, however, serious-looking men strode about, issuing commands and debating strategy.

"We run war games," Chambers confirmed, "to test defences, anticipate problems, and determine the best strategies to use. Our biggest challenge lies in anticipating the Martian behaviours. No-one here has witnessed them in action, and the few military men who did... Well, they had only a limited perspective, seeing the fight from one location. Your book," he added, "has been our manual — but we hope you can provide a fresh insight into their activities."

"You wish me to play games with you?" I said.

Chambers laughed. "In fact, yes. If any man alive is best placed to put himself in the minds of the enemy, it will be you."

I shuddered. If I had no desire to relive those days hiding from the invaders, I had still less to divine their thoughts. Chambers sensed my hesitancy.

"We have devised tactics, and the army are running drills to test themselves and our equipment — but the grander view, a suitable strategy, eludes us. Where to deploy our men, how to anticipate the Martians' advances, here we are blind. These games have a serious purpose, and you will help us immensely. I do not intend to put you into the field, you will be safe here educating us."

"I suppose I can offer what insight I might have," I conceded. "I assume you wish to start with a recreation of the events around Woking?" I gestured to the map.

He nodded. "At first, yes, we might tease out some of their thinking that way, but soon we will move on to scenarios designed to test our new equipment against them."

"You have weapons? New devices to stop them?" My excitement quite overtook me, and I saw my brother suppress a smile as he spoke.

"Not here, but if that would interest you I could arrange a demonstration one day?"

I had never much been interested in the weapons of war; in youth, my peers had played with toy soldiers reenacting famous battles of history while I had preferred the company and education of books. Now I would fill that gap in my childhood experiences to a more noble purpose. I was about to answer in the affirmative when a dishevelled courier arrived at the door, panting and clutching a slip of paper. Frederick took it, and his face paled as he read.

"Flashes seen on Mars."

<hr />

Telescopes around the world were constantly trained on the fourth planet and had been since the events of two years prior. As soon as the flashes of the giant launching guns appeared, telegraph signals encircled the world with the news. The realisation that the long-feared second coming was already under way shattered the peace of that crisp autumn afternoon.

I had to return home. While it would be at least ten days before the Martians could arrive, Amy would be concerned for my wellbeing, and I had no business here that couldn't wait. "Is the news common knowledge?" I asked.

Frederick assured me that they would make no official announcement for another hour, but noted that rumours had a way of spreading, and agreed I should not wait too long. I bid him and Chambers farewell and good luck and headed for home.

Making my way across town towards Whitehall, I saw a few people forming queues outside the banks as people tried to withdraw any savings or funds that they could. Shops were being stripped bare of supplies as people learned of the developments, and passed on the news to their neighbours once they themselves had stocked up. My pace increased along with my anxiety.

Upon arrival to Waterloo, the concourse heaved with passengers seeking a route to any point outside of the capital where they might feel safer. I could not see the ticket offices for the mass of people, and I heard voices raised in anger from all sides. I made my way towards the platform as quickly as I could.

A giant crowd thronged the platform and besieged my train. Each man, woman and child among them was heavily laden with bags, suitcases and parcels and they jostled one another as they pressed towards the train doors. The guards were struggling to restrain them as the incoming passengers alighted, and minor scuffles broke out. I had the luxury of a first-class ticket, and by some good fortune the crowd had not yet descended so low as to disregard classes entirely. I could thus board without forcing my way through.

The train made its way through the countryside towards Woking, and wherever it passed a road, I witnessed people fleeing just as they had in the first invasion. There were belongings piled on carts, animals or just carried on the backs of the evacuees. No doubt they had decided that it was not worth waiting to see whether the Martians were indeed coming here or had decided to try Venus.

A newspaper vendor at Woking station had a little more information. By then the news had broken, and a telegraph message had been hurriedly printed onto newsprint. I bought a copy for a penny and read what little we knew so far. The first flashes had been seen almost as soon as the sun had set the night before, and thirty-seven had been counted before Mars sank below the horizon. And all this on one night! If they continued this rate, we might face an invasion many times larger in its audacity than the last. In this sparse page the government had appealed for calm, assured the population that everything was in hand, and introduced rationing of essentials effective immediately.

As might have been predicted, these reassurances elicited the precisely opposite effect to that which had been intended. I felt my own sense of panic returning even as I read. In vain did the shopkeepers of Woking try to limit the worst excesses of panic buying, reminding the worried populace that the Martians had to be at least ten days' travel away.

Fist fights had even broken out at the general store near the station when bread and milk ran out, and by the time I arrived there the proprietor was nursing what would develop into a shiner of a black eye by the next morning.

I witnessed the ineffectiveness of the appeal for calm as I walked through the newly rebuilt centre of Woking. Most of the houses destroyed in the first invasion were repaired or rebuilt by this time, only a few empty plots remaining as evidence of the destruction. And yet there was a reminder of that fateful period all around me, as men and women ran here and there in a panic, clutching armfuls of provisions. When I stopped one particularly harried-looking man and enquired what was the matter, he looked at me as if I had just crawled out from under a rock.

"The Martians!" he gasped. "They're coming!" With that he ran off, leaving a trail of dropped tins and lavatory paper behind himself.

To witness the collapse of natural decorum was startling enough, but following such indifference and disinterest as I had witnessed felt like a betrayal.

Chapter Four

Panic

As I turned the corner onto my road, Amy stood at the garden gate, peering along the street. When she caught sight of me, she ran to meet me, skirts billowing behind her. She caught me in a tight embrace, fairly knocking the wind out of me. I extricated myself after a few moments, conscious of the eyes of our neighbours upon us, and we walked back towards the house.

"Are you well?" I enquired. "Has there been any danger to you here?" The street was silent compared to the crush of the town centre.

She shook her head. "The trouble was all in town," she told me. "A few folks have run about in panic, some seem to have left for good, but I was more worried for you."

"I can take care of myself quite well, thank you," I replied with a smile.

"Being caught up in a crowd in London, I quite feared it would have reminded you of the last time. I'm glad I was wrong, you seem quite yourself. I take it Frederick had good news for you?" We arrived home and closed the door behind us.

"Indeed, he did. Preparations are underway, and my words of caution and advice have been heeded, at least by some." I outlined what I had seen of their work, and she embraced me once more with relief. "That has certainly reassured me, but most helpful was finding that I could assist them." I felt Amy's shoulders tensing again under my arms, but I pressed on. "Mostly by letter-writing and support-gathering, as I have been already."

She broke the embrace and regarded me sternly. "And you believe a few letters and speeches will have a bigger effect than this morning's news? The panic you see in the streets is the population taking this as seriously as can be. What might you add to that?" I hesitated. "What have you agreed to?" she demanded.

I explained my brother's idea of assisting with battle plans and strategies. I outlined Chambers' reasoning, that my experiences in the first invasion were unparalleled, that I might have witnessed something, however small, which could prove helpful to our defence. My protests fell on deaf ears.

"You are to play at toy soldiers while the very threat you feared approaches?" She paced around the kitchen. "Worse than that, you intend to revisit those days of horror once more and examine the misery and despair we have worked so hard to exorcise from you? What benefit can this have for them? Do you fancy yourself a more capable tactician than a Field Marshall?" Tears sprang to her eyes, and I stepped towards her, my arms outstretched. She dashed them away angrily. "If we had a spell of years, perhaps you might have advised them in some manner. But now it is a matter of weeks, days even, and you would leave me to fend for myself while you live out some half-baked dream of winning a battle you lost long ago?"

Her words stung. Amy knew better than anyone what horrors I had experienced in that first invasion. She had never used my breakdown or my experiences against me before. Protests rose in my mind, arguments to change her mind. I wanted to explain, to force her into understanding why I needed this, but the words died on my lips when I realised the anger on her face was tempered by concern and love. She had been my only ally during those dark days, and if she appeared to turn on me now, it was only out of fear that something might hurt me again.

And I shared that fear. "I would never leave you, my greatest distress in that first conflict was believing that I had lost you. My greatest joy was the day of our reunion. And they have promised us a place with them, a safe refuge when the Martians come. There we will be secure, and protected."

"I wish to heavens that your brother had just told you all was well, and let you come back to me with peace in your heart. Why did the fool have to fill your head with ideas of assisting, and keep this ridiculous notion alive?"

For all the public's supposed belief in our superiority and inevitable victory, their reaction to the news of the Martians' return was far from calm and philosophical. Their confidence was exposed as only skin-deep; most people were terrified and preferred to ignore the possibility of a return rather than face it. Stores across the nation rapidly ran low on essential supplies as people stockpiled provisions in panic; the commandeering of transport and delivery vehicles for military purposes compounded the shortages. Even Amy had to agree that my policy of buying a couple of extra, non-perishable items each time we replenished the larder had been sensible, and she was glad she had heeded my suggestion to pickle and preserve what we could. This last had been especially prudent as those of us who had planted fruits and vegetables found them raided at night and stripped bare of even the under-ripened produce. At least my foresight meant that we did not need to go hungry.

With no forward planning, rationing proved almost impossible to implement fairly. In smaller towns, shopkeepers knew their customers well enough to identify anyone buying more than their fair share, though they turned a blind eye to all but the most egregious of stockpilers. In larger places where the rations might be more strictly observed, it was easier for the greedy to send out each member of the family to buy additional quotas, or to give a false name and address to circumvent any restrictions. By any of these methods, the shelves were emptied in short order.

I heard tell of runs on the banks in London and elsewhere, as people withdrew their savings. Pawn-brokers reported that gold and silver jewellery were in high demand as a means of carrying wealth. No doubt the pick-pockets also enjoyed an increase in their nefarious business as a result.

And all of this began the very night that the first flashes occurred — despite it being expected that the cylinders would take ten days to make their journey, much as before. It might take slightly longer as the distance to Mars at this opposition was a fraction greater, but certainly they could not arrive sooner. There was, therefore, a lengthy period after we witnessed the launches, with nothing to do but wait in growing fear. Human nature was not equal to the task of quiet contemplation and preparation in the face of impending attack.

Soldiers mobilised nationwide, with a particular concentration in the South-East of the country, and I frequently caught sight of them drilling as I cycled across the Surrey hills. Trains delivered large artillery guns through Woking, two unloaded there and transported to the sand pits, while others passed through bound for all corners of the country.

Several people boarded up their homes and set off out of town — some headed North while others made for the English Channel and the Continent, no doubt believing that we could expect a repeat of the previous assault and only the London environs would see occupation. The ferries to France departed crammed with people, but within the day they were returning as they had left, the passengers reporting they had been refused permission to disembark.

Our neighbours were closing the gates on us.

Questions were asked in the House of Commons, and it forced the Secretary of State for Foreign Affairs to make a statement on the matter. He reported that the Nations of Europe had quite enough of their own problems considering the Martian's impending return, and that they were not equipped to deal with a refugee exodus from our shores. He also stated that we ourselves would not be accepting any overseas visitors ourselves "until the current crisis is resolved." I suspected our neighbours were unwilling to assist because of our government's own policy of non-cooperation over sharing of the spoils of war, though perhaps owing to the rules of diplomacy no such suggestion was ever publicly made.

The less reputable of the newspapers slandered our foreign cousins as they so often did, printing outrageous stories with limited, if any, truth to them, which fanned the flames of xenophobia still further. When one tabloid printed an illustration depicting the French President kissing the feet of a tripod and gesturing towards the White Cliffs of Dover, a mob surrounded the Embassy of France and horse-mounted police charged to break it up.

Panic spread to every aspect of life in those tense, waiting days. Churches overflowed with even those who had never set foot in one before seeking absolution or divine intervention. Crowds thronged in parks and fields to listen to the clergy urging compassion and gentleness, then surged into towns to pick over already-looted shops and fight one another for meagre supplies. Others eagerly devoured the doom-mongering of the self appointed 'Prophets of the Martians' who experienced a remarkable rise in their popularity now that their pronouncements had an element of truth behind them.

In some of the largest cities, the army had to halt their preparations and assist the police in regaining order. The first casualties of the second Martian invasion were in fact killed at the hands of their fellow man, when the military fired upon an angry mob in Leicester. This action did not get widely reported, the disruption to the newspapers and communications working to the benefit of the authorities in that regard. Only those who were there knew of what happened, and any reports which reached the wider country were lost amidst a tidal wave of misinformation, exaggeration, and downright lies. I only knew of it because of my own contacts with the government through my brother. Doubtless, there were many more of these incidents across the nation and indeed the world, though considering subsequent events, those lives lost were barely a fraction.

Woking itself was not as badly affected as most places. Perhaps it was to do with having already faced the adversary before, perhaps the town's smaller size and status as a dormitory town for the metropolis saved it from the excesses of humanity at its worst. I do not flatter myself that my own efforts had any effect on my town's reaction to the imminent threat. Not that our lives were not disrupted, with the trains commandeered and food in short supply, but I consider us fortunate compared to others.

After a couple of days, with those residents who wished to flee having found somewhere to go or returning with their tails between their legs, Woking and the country at large returned to something approaching normality again. Supplies were getting through once more, the army having finished their initial manoeuvres. Before the week was out, and with full bellies, the public lost their appetite for trouble and showed every sign of embarrassment at their temporary outburst. An uneasy calm settled over the nation, though tempers were still short. Every man gazed heaven-wards countless times a day, in fear of a Martian cylinder coming down at any moment. Each night brought reports of more flashes on the surface of the red planet, more cylinders launched towards us.

As is so often the case in such times, a macabre sense of humour surfaced. The landlord of the Spotted Dog took wagers each evening on how many flashes would be reported in the morning papers.

Most of us just carried on as close to a normal life as possible, and there were even periods when each of us forgot for a moment that the brief calm around us would not last.

Meanwhile, preparations were still ongoing. The government announced that gas masks would be issued to protect against the effects of the Black Smoke. When the first ones were issued, they turned out to leak poorly around the face because of inferior rubber being used.

An acquaintance of my brother's who frequented the right London club informed us that the gossip there among government men was that our Indian plantations were refusing to export their crop to us. All shipments of goods from the sub-continent had in fact been blocked until suitable assurances of protection from the Martians were received. Attempts to source rubber from elsewhere were being blocked by the Government of Belgium, who controlled the production in the Congo, perhaps in protest at what they perceived as the British keeping a monopoly on Martian technology. Nevertheless, a new source was evidently secured, as later deliveries of the gas masks were of a higher quality. Only a strictly limited number emerged, however, and so only residents of the larger cities and industrial centres received any, and that only after the army.

None of this troubled the population at all, in fact the man in the street would be unlikely to have heard about the troubles in India — if he did, his concern would most likely be over any interruption to the tea supply, rather than protective equipment. When the last shipments of the masks arrived at civic centres, most went unclaimed, and I believe that most of those who had picked them up looked at them more as souvenirs or knick-knacks than something meant for their safety. Certainly, when the time came that they were needed, very few saw service.

The press made only brief mention of any of this, ostensibly to prevent panic among the populace. I doubt most of the public would have even noticed if the government had been completely open about the situation, but there were still a handful of individuals who felt that the establishment was hiding the truth for their own reasons. In the absence of clear factual information, speculation ran rife, and bizarre theories spread like wildfire. There were no Martians, the government merely using the threat to 'keep us all in line'. It was a plot by our adversaries to mask their own military aspirations (variously rumoured to be the French, German or Spanish governments, depending on who told the tale). Our government intended to sell us into slavery to the Martians in exchange for some unknown benefit. One rumour even claimed that the Martians had been here since the first invasion, alive and well, and were running everything behind the scenes. I met no one who claimed to believe any of these ludicrous ideas, and yet I heard them at every turn. More credible were those rumours that the preparations were inadequate and the secrecy was merely to ensure that our last days as the superior species on the planet were not spent in rioting. Mere arguments would not convince those who would believe in such conspiracies, so I did not waste my time on them.

As the clocks ticked the time away, church bells were silenced, their chimes reserved for warning of the arrival. Even this small disruption left many of us disoriented, I for one had not realised how much I relied on the tolling from a distant steeple to mark the passing of the day. Frequently I realised hours had passed seemingly without my realising, and yet the days dragged slowly by. Even the rising and setting of the sun did not bring enough order to the day, and my sense of disconnection grew as the predicted date of arrival came ever closer.

This did not stop the more excitable elements among the population from jumping at every unexplained sound, or spreading rumours of a cylinder landing nearby. Each time a sighting was reported, it had apparently come from a trusted friend of the storyteller, or a friend of a family member — and each time it failed to be true. When a storm hit the South-East late one night, every distant crash of thunder announced the arrival of a cylinder to those more credulous individuals. The following morning saw a giant crowd gather at the pit where the first cylinder had fallen two years previously, just to reassure themselves that nothing had appeared overnight.

Among their number had been the proprietor of the Spotted Dog, who recounted to me that evening his impressions of the assembly.

"We were relieved, of course," he said across the bar. "Not that we can't take care of 'em, of course," he gestured to a handful of soldiers in the snug, "but maybe it's someone else's turn to have 'em on their doorsteps."

The patrons murmured their agreement.

"If you ask me, some of 'em were disappointed," one man spoke up. "Like they was hoping to see 'em again." His audience met this with general incredulity.

"No one as saw 'em first time round would want to again, ain't that right?" the barman said to me.

However, this impression of a group of people who might well wish to see the Martians again had stuck with me. I recalled the man at Speaker's Corner, depicting the invaders as a cleansing agent for the sins of mankind. Then there were the 'Prophets' and I wondered if their words had found fertile ground nearby. I resolved to find out for myself.

Chapter Five

Common

So it was that I found myself on Horsell Common once more. I had avoided this general area since the events of the first invasion, and I found my feet oddly reluctant to bring me back this way now.

The trees on the common were short and stunted, fresh growth having not yet replaced what the touch of the heat-ray had consumed. Low shrubs had taken advantage of the clearing and threatened to trip me, but a well-trodden path led me safely through the worst of it. The birdsong I usually heard in the Surrey countryside was absent — whether because the local population were yet to recover from the battle, or because they had been disturbed by the army's emplacing of their guns, I did not know.

I encountered a small group of people at the edge of the crater where the first cylinder had arrived, gazing down thoughtfully into it. A small marker sat at the rim in memory of those first victims of the invasion, and they thronged about it. As I drew nearer, one of their number turned to face me.

"Hullo!" he called, with a wave.

"Good morning!" I called back. Their clothing looked strange to me; stout boots made sense given the uneven terrain, as did the jodhpurs they wore, but their shirts were long and shift-like, and none wore tie or jacket. All were hatless and wore their hair cropped short.

"Have you come to pay respect?" another of the men asked as I joined them.

I felt it prudent to agree, though it was not my true motive. I looked down into the pit where it all began. The army had removed the cylinder as soon as the battle was over; now the gouge in the earth it made was part-filled with water after the storm, the sand unable to drain after our wet summer. I stood in thought for a few moments; the group seemed unwilling to disturb my meditation.

When I looked up, I regarded them through watery eyes. A woman dressed as the others were in jodhpurs and shirt, with hair cropped short, also enquired if I was unwell, and whether I was mourning a loss in the attack.

"No, not I — although it was a close-run thing," I replied, and explained my experiences. When the group realised I was the author of the popular account of the invasion, they brightened considerably and peppered me with questions.

Where had I been when the cylinder landed? What had I done when I heard of it? What were my impressions of the Martians upon first sighting them? And a dozen other, most of which I had already expounded upon at length in my account. I did my best to answer, and then they moved on to enquiries that I had not addressed before.

What had the Martian's motives been? Had they taken pleasure in their activities, showed signs of satisfaction? Was it possible to tell what they had thought, what they truly wanted? Did I feel their purpose was unfulfilled by their untimely demise?

Under this onslaught, one query overlapping another, I came to realise a peculiar pattern. Their questions might be innocent enough, many of us wondered what the purpose of the invasion had been. But their eagerness and enthusiasm gave me the distinct impression that in their minds the greatest tragedy had not been the arrival of the Martians, nor their decimation of the landscape and its inhabitants, but the failure of the invasion. In fact, it occurred to me that their sympathies lay with the invaders. They did indeed seem to be related in outlook to the man at Speaker's Corner, if not more enthusiastic. I had no time for this viewpoint.

"Let me be clear," I said, using the declaratory voice I employed in my short tenure as a teacher. "The Martians are no friends of ours, nor an adversary that reason can deter. Violence is the only solution."

"But they are children of God, are they not?" one of the group asked.

I was in no mood for a debate. "I do not know if they are part of God's creation, but I can assure you all that I saw no hint of His mercy in their actions."

"Ah, but was it not God's mercy which flooded the world? When He burned Sodom and Gomorrah, was it not done out of love? He cleanses us of our sins, as Peter said: *The coming of the day of God, wherein the heavens being on fire shall be dissolved, and the elements shall melt with fervent heat? Nevertheless we, according to his promise, look for new heavens and a new Earth, wherein dwelleth righteousness."*

I stood there a moment before I found my voice. "They are mere creatures, not gods. Intelligent, yes, but no more than we ourselves. This planet is ours as Mars is theirs, and it should remain that way."

The woman spoke now. "We have proven ourselves unworthy of this Earth, this Eden. Our sins will be counted and we will be found wanting." Her words were well-rehearsed, almost chanted.

I rounded on her. "The Martians are invaders, not messengers of God. They are not coming here to judge us, to weigh our hearts against a feather or make us pass through a needle's eye. They are coming here to take our home and our lives from us."

Their leader continued. "Those who are free of sin will be spared and taken up into Heaven to watch the wickedness end."

"You believe they will spare you? Take you up into space to watch the Earth burn?"

The others then began reciting another bible verse. *"Therefore hath the curse devoured the Earth, and they that dwell therein are desolate: therefore the inhabitants of the Earth are burned, and few men left."*

They continued in this vein, brandishing bibles and (it horrified me to see) copies of my own account as I fled the scene. The last sight I had of them as I hurried away was of them reaching skywards, calling down the holy, cleansing fire.

———◆◇◆———

I returned home in dour spirits. My mood lifted when I was met by a telegram inviting me to witness our preparations, as Chambers and Frederick had promised. The reader will understand my enthusiasm for seeing with my own eyes that our government was in fact taking our concerns seriously, and so I hurriedly wrote a reply agreeing to visit the next day. I should have expected that Amy would reject this proposal.

"Stay here," she urged me. "They can manage perfectly well without you."

"I must go, if only to lay my fears to rest," I protested. "Witnessing their preparations first-hand will be helpful to me. And this journey will allow me to see the place where we are to be safe. You will be fine here, everyone is calm now and there is nothing to fear."

"I'm not concerned for myself," she said. "The latest estimates don't have them arriving until Saturday. I just don't understand why you cannot wait until we are both able to travel there together.

For that matter, why can we not both go there now? If they intend us to be safe, why not have us there well before the arrival, rather than leaving it so late?"

I had been entertaining thoughts along those lines myself, and in my darker moments had even worried if the offer of sanctuary was merely a ruse to stop me from making too much fuss. I trusted my brother, however, and believed that he would never have extended such an offer if he did not believe it to be genuine. Still, seeing him and Chambers face to face would allow me to verify the truth of the situation for myself. I just needed to explain this to Amy without alarming her.

"You don't trust them," Amy said, guessing my thoughts. "That's why, isn't it? You believe that if you're right there in front of them, they won't be able to refuse you? All the more reason for me to accompany you then."

"It isn't quite that simple. It's a top-secret research establishment, and they won't allow..." I hesitated.

"Women?" Amy asked.

"Anyone not invited," I finished. "They have asked me to help, and you know I intend to do so. But what would you have me do, take it all on trust and sit here in my armchair while the threat grows ever closer?"

"Of course not," she smiled. "I would have you tear up that reply, and write a new telegram asking for explicit instructions for reaching this place of safety. We can then set out as soon as it arrives, together."

Why had I not thought of such an approach myself? Rather than agonising over the truth or otherwise behind their words, I could have simply asked them for the details from the start. I sat at my desk, wrote a brief telegram explaining that I could not attend but would appreciate the immediate forwarding of details for the evacuation. Amy read over my brief note, nodded in approval, and set off to the post office to send it immediately.

<hr />

The following morning brought no reply. My breakfast was ashes in my mouth as my fears grew. Had I been misled? Had my own brother lied to me about an opportunity for salvation, or had he himself been deceived? Were we destined to die in our home, or scatter across the country as we had the previous time, only to risk separation and loss?

With each passing hour without the telegram boy's knock at the door, my heart sank further. I could barely meet Amy's eyes and confined myself to my office to avoid her. She could not have believed that I was writing, not now, but she did not invade my privacy. While I know she would never have blamed me for the situation, I could not help but bear the guilt of giving her such false hope.

I paced the floor in front of my desk, my mind in turmoil. We had but two days until the Martians' expected arrival, at best, and I had to accept that help was not coming.

I had to make a plan for us now, all the weight was upon my shoulders. I pored over my collection of local maps in search of some ideal hiding spot; perhaps a cave or an old mine or quarry would do the trick. Anyone familiar with the Surrey countryside would know as well as I did it was a fruitless search. Nothing of the sort existed within easy reach, and I could hardly bear the idea of Amy living in a hole in the ground. Not for the first time I cursed myself for not excavating a basement beneath our house during the past two years, but with all available workmen being employed rebuilding housing, an opportunity had not really presented itself.

How far could we cycle in a day, I wondered? On our occasional trips out, we had never covered more than around ten miles, but properly prepared and with the right motivation, I was sure we could both cover double that. I drew a circle of that radius around Woking and examined the area within as closely as the map's level of detail allowed.

I am not sure how long I was engaged in that activity before a cheerful whistle from the street outside distracted me. Stretching my aching back, and curious who might be in such good spirits on such a miserable day, I crossed to the window and peered out.

The telegram boy! In his smart jacket and hat he practically skipped along the road towards our house. I threw open my office door, hurtled down the stairs and hauled open the front door with such speed that the poor boy almost jumped out of his skin.

"Lawks, sir, you startled me! Telegram for you, sir," he said, holding out the flimsy piece of paper. I snatched it from his grasp, tipped him a shilling, and slammed the door back shut. Hands trembling, I tore open the envelope and scanned the message within.

BROOKWOOD. PASSWORD PHOBOS. DETAILS FOLLOW BY MAIL.

I collapsed into a chair, heart pounding in my ears. There was a plan.

---------------◀◇▶---------------

With a goal to aim towards, I found my mind was much calmer. I almost laughed as we set to work packing such necessities as we could not manage without. Amy grumbled that they might have provided us with more information to make this task easier.

"Even some idea of the laundry facilities would be useful. How many clothes should we take? What of food, kitchen equipment?"

"I am sure they will provide for all our needs," I assured her. "And when the promised instructions arrive by post, we will shall know more."

"You expect me to believe that the necropolis has all the conveniences of modern life?" Amy asked, trying unsuccessfully to fold one of my shirts into a small overnight bag without creasing it. "Or are we to inhabit one of the mausolea and not care for our appearance?"

There may be some readers who are unfamiliar with the cemetery at Brookwood, or the London Necropolis, as it is officially named. As the capital outgrew its historic graveyards, a new one was established a few miles from Woking with regular train services to ferry the dead and their mourners. It was the largest cemetery in the world, and they had given a section over to the casualties of the first invasion. Was it possible that there was a hidden sanctuary, perhaps constructed along with the mass graves of those nameless unfortunates? I shuddered at the idea of cowering among the dead, but felt it unlikely.

"Our final destination shall not be there," I stated confidently. "The government could not have been performing their research at such a well-known location with secrecy. I suspect it is merely the local rallying point for our evacuation to somewhere much safer."

"I'm bringing potted meat," Amy said as her only reply. "Whether or not we are to squat among the dead, we shall need food. And I do not trust your friends to have made adequate provision." She placed a selection of our stockpiled tinned goods into the base of a second bag, testing its weight as she did so. "I shall bake bread this evening," she decided, "it's light but filling, and will travel well."

I marvelled at her composure. I had been on the verge of panic attempting to decide what to do, and here she was planning our meals and preparing for any eventuality. Once again, I counted myself lucky to have her in my life. I recalled how close we had come to losing one another before, and how deeply that had affected me. I remembered her kindness and compassion when I stumbled home in a daze, haunted by the things I had seen and done, and her unquestioning acceptance of the necessity of my actions. Most of all, I cherished her support and care when the dark moods took hold, when those impulses that had driven me to stand before the Martian war machine and plead for it to take me had returned. Only the death of the invaders had spared me. To what purpose I could not know, I was sure I did not deserve such forgiveness, but with her help, I had rebuilt the life I had now.

And it was all about to come crashing down.

Chapter Six

Arrival

The first cylinder landed in the early hours of the following morning, a few miles outside Manchester. Reports from that night are patchy and incomplete, but I have pieced together what I later learned.

The skies being under constant surveillance meant that the fiery descent of the Martians was immediately spotted and reported. Church bells across the southern edge of the city rang out in warning and woke all those who would find themselves in the same vicinity as the arrival. Most fled, but despite the chilly night, the crater dug by the cylinder's landing was quickly surrounded by a mix of curiosity seekers, self-appointed 'keepers of the peace' and the more enterprising members of society who always insert themselves into proceedings and distribute hot drinks and foods for a nominal fee. There was also a journalist from the *Manchester Evening News*, from whom most of this information came.

The army had been patrolling there as elsewhere, in small groups. The few soldiers first on the scene found themselves outnumbered by the public, and being unwilling to open fire upon civilians, were quickly overwhelmed. Before long, improvised weapons were being used by the crowd to bludgeon or pry the cylinder open, to little effect other than preventing the military from taking control. Scuffles broke out between those who wanted to drag the Martians from their capsule and hang them, and those who preferred to welcome them to our planet. With the arrival of reinforcements, the army established a perimeter, and the guns moved up into position. Once the crowd was driven back sufficiently, the first field gun fired a ranging shot, and upon the confirmation of their accuracy, they opened fire.

Five rounds fell on the invaders in rapid succession, each to the accompaniment of a cheer from the assembled mass, and boos from the believers. Smoke and dust filled the air for some time, and when it cleared, a bank of newly arrived electrical lights switched on to aid inspection. A handful of troops marched forward to inspect the damage, while the rest of their number fought to restrain the crowd.

Those first to the lip of the crater were immediately immolated by the heat-ray.

General panic overtook the crowd, who scattered in all directions. The artillery piece fired additional rounds, but with the benefit of illumination it was now apparent that the projectiles were exploding some distance above the Martians. The dust and debris thrown up by the explosions were not falling back into the pit but settling in a ring around the edge. A shimmering haze lay over the cylinder and the gouge it had made, shielding the occupants from harm.

The heat-ray projector emerged from the cylinder once more and laid waste to its surroundings, burning men and machinery together as it flickered across the terrain. The artillery continued to fire from its hidden location long after the futility of it became clear. It is to the credit of our army that the brave men who stood there continued fighting until the last man, as their rounds pinged off the shield and their comrades-in-arms fell beside them.

By the time dawn came, not a single human was alive within half a mile. Those who had not fled were destroyed utterly.

During that terrible night, a dozen cylinders rained down over Britain, and as we later discovered, the rest of Europe too. The Martians had clearly learned from their prior failure. Not only had they provided shielding for each of the arriving ships, but they had also landed many more of them much more rapidly and more widely than before. This latter tactic stretched us thin — with most of the army deployed across the Southern stretches of the country, the further North the Martians landed the less resistance they faced.

We shall never know how many people died that first night, but it must have been tens of thousands. In each location, the same hideous scene played out, except for two. In Scotland, the cylinder aimed at Edinburgh was successfully destroyed, presumably because of a malfunction in their shield. By the time the twelfth and final cylinder of that night landed near Staines, word had reached the locals of the fate of the others and no crowd gathered to watch the battle. The army held their distance, raining down shells from all sides to little effect.

I have never been much for early mornings, preferring to enjoy breakfast and a pot of tea before beginning my day. That morning, a prolonged and piercing whistle from the street outside awoke me, which did more for my alertness than any breakfast could have. On investigating, I found one of the local policemen who was informing each road in turn about the arrival of the Martians.

"Remain calm, stay home, and await further instructions," he called out as he paced the pavement outside. Another long shrill blast on the whistle, and then another call a few houses along. Few were heeding his instructions, and most gathered in small groups to discuss the events of the night, while others evacuated the town.

I learned a little more from a newspaper seller who followed in the policeman's wake. Details were still vague at that point, but any lingering belief among the populace in our superiority and inevitable victory had been sorely tested. Throughout that day various reports would come in to flesh out the picture, along with rumours of other landings and similar destruction. I later heard tell that as news spread, a stampede had begun towards the train station, a tidal wave of bodies swamping the main gates. Unfortunately for those in the vanguard, the army had suspended the train service minutes before to allow for the freer movement of soldiers, and the gates to the platforms were chained shut. Those following behind, unaware of this, pressed forward allowing no retreat and crushed their fellows against the steel. The poor station staff attempted to reason with the mob, to explain that no trains were to stop here, and eventually the manager had little option but to draw a pistol and fire above their heads in warning.

This did little to calm matters, but did at least startle several of the crowd sufficiently to drive them back and relieve the pressure, too late for those unfortunates who had led the way. In the meantime, a steady stream of individuals and families thronged the roads out of Woking, heading in any direction that might offer safety.

Amy and I had already grabbed our bags to make haste out of the town. While we might have hoped for the additional evacuation details my brother had promised, it seemed unlikely in the extreme that the postal service would still be running. We would simply have to make do with the sparse instructions from the telegram we had received. Thus it was that Amy and I made our way towards Brookwood, almost four miles outside town. We made use of our bicycles, strapping our bags to the panniers and joining the flow of pedestrians towards the countryside. Each was heavily laden with belongings; many had pressed carts and wheelbarrows into service as makeshift luggage trolleys.

Once or twice someone would try to hail us, which we ignored, and one harried-looking man stepped into the road to stop me. The idea that he would knock me over and steal my bicycle terrified me, but I swerved around him at the last minute and aimed a kick at his knee. It connected and while I wobbled slightly before regaining my balance; he fell. His curses followed Amy and me down the street, but he soon fell out of earshot behind us.

The first cylinder I witnessed with my own eyes came down near Guildford, streaking overhead as we passed the golf course. Of course I was not alone in this observation — the entire mass of people upon the road came to a stand-still, eyes turned to the sky as the giant glowing fireball passed silently. As it disappeared over the horizon, leaving behind a roiling black trail of smoke, a deafening crash shook the earth around us and broke the spell. I suspected that this was the sound of it thundering through the air, but most people assumed it was the impact with the land. "It's hit, it's hit!" people cried out, and ran in all directions. Amy and I were roughly jostled and almost separated from our bicycles as the panic spread. We clung tight to one another and our means of transport until the crowds thinned enough to allow us to proceed. We pressed on cautiously, always alert to the risk of someone assaulting us, and were glad when we turned aside from the main road and took a less crowded path towards Brookwood.

The village of Brookwood had its own station, but this was now locked up tight. We did not stop there, once we noted the gates were drawn and locked, lest the small but anxious crowd there took a fancy to our bicycles. We pulled up on a deserted side road to catch our breath, where a few houses stood with their front doors wide open, evidently abandoned in haste.

Amy drank deeply from the water she had packed. "Surely the military has expected and planned for their commandeering of the railways, and the key stations being closed," she remarked. "So it really must be the cemetery to which that telegram referred." She passed me the water, and I realised how thirsty I was. I found I was shaking so much I spilt almost as much as I drank.

"I assume so," I said. "And there is a station there if it's not our ultimate destination."

"Might that not be closed also?"

That had been my fear as well, though I did not want to worry her unduly. "It's a spur line, and no-one has ever started a journey at the graveside, so the locals might overlook it." Her expression told me she didn't really believe my explanation, but we had very little other choice.

We shared some of the bread Amy had baked the previous night, and consulted the map. We headed out along the Bagshot road, which skirted the Necropolis. Suitably refreshed and with a more concrete aim in mind, I felt my mood lifting slightly, and we set off again.

A short while later, we arrived at the high brick wall that encircled the place. After following this structure, keeping it on our left for about a half a mile, we came across a tall steel gate. Stood in front of it was a fidgety corporal who fingered his pistol in its holster anxiously as we stopped and dismounted. He was younger than either Amy or me and looked barely old enough to have enlisted.

"Hullo!" I called cheerfully, and waved, which did nothing to calm him. His eyes darted between my wife and I, as if trying to determine if we were Martians in disguise. I gave my name, and the code-word 'Phobos', and he relaxed slightly. He took his hand from his pistol's hilt, fumbled a sheet of paper from his greatcoat pocket and checked it, his eyes flitting up at us constantly. He found my name, nodded, and tucked the paper away again.

He took a deep breath. "Head for the Anglican Cemetery," he said as he unlocked the gate. He checked both directions up the road before pulling it open. "Then make your way to the South Cemetery Station." We stepped through the gate and he locked it quickly behind us. "Good luck."

"And to you," I replied, before we took our leave of him.

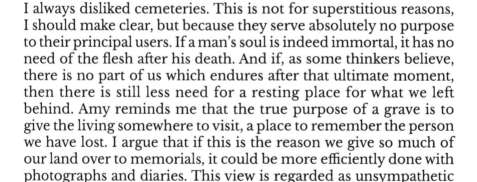

I always disliked cemeteries. This is not for superstitious reasons, I should make clear, but because they serve absolutely no purpose to their principal users. If a man's soul is indeed immortal, it has no need of the flesh after his death. And if, as some thinkers believe, there is no part of us which endures after that ultimate moment, then there is still less need for a resting place for what we left behind. Amy reminds me that the true purpose of a grave is to give the living somewhere to visit, a place to remember the person we have lost. I argue that if this is the reason we give so much of our land over to memorials, it could be more efficiently done with photographs and diaries. This view is regarded as unsympathetic by many, and I have learned to avoid sharing it.

Whatever the reasons for my distaste, the low mist that clung around the stubs of gravestones lent an eerie air to the place. It was thicker in the tree-screened area that held the mass graves which had been nicknamed 'Martian Hollow'. Our steps quickened as we passed by.

The so-called station was merely a raised concrete platform beside the single track, a couple of benches upon it, and a wooden fence at the rear. There were many men in army uniforms at one end. Some paced nervously, but most sat cross-legged or with their feet dangling over the side of the platform. They had rifles slung over their backs, ammunition in pouches attached to their belts and almost to a man were smoking cigarettes. Towards the nearer end of the station were the civilians. There were barely twenty of us in total. The men all seemed to know one another and were conversing agitatedly in low voices. The few women were tending to a handful of children, endeavouring to keep them entertained and, no doubt, also distracting themselves from the experiences of the morning. As Amy and I mounted the few steps to the platform, several faces turned in our direction, but they deemed us to be of little interest, and people went back to their previous activities.

One individual showed some reaction to our arrival. He stood up with clear difficulty and waved us over. I recognised a tired-looking Chambers and noticed a grubby plaster cast on his left arm. Someone had torn his jacket sleeve to allow this through, and the rest of his clothes looked crumpled and dusty. As we approached, he sat back heavily on the bench with a groan. Sat beside him was a worried-looking woman I took to be his wife, and two small children who clung to her skirts and avoided my eye.

"What the devil are you doing here?" I asked him.

"I was up in London yesterday for some last-minute preparations, and to collect the family," he gestured at the people beside himself. "The Prime Minister wanted a briefing on our readiness. Once that was done, there were already rumours of the first landings, and I found myself caught up in a riot," he said, showing the cast on his arm. "Once the medics had put this right, the last trains were already leaving. We cadged a lift this far, and were forced to try and sleep on this bench. Now I'm itching to get to work."

"What do you know of the situation?" I asked. "You must know more than I."

He shook his head. "Little enough," he admitted. "It's worse than we feared, that much is clear. But this must be your wife?"

I introduced her, apologising for my lack of manners, and he reciprocated before another of Chambers' colleagues joined us.

"Our train is coming," he informed us, and we made our way to the edge of the short platform. The sergeant called the soldiers to order, and they grumbled as they rose to their feet. An engine pulling a trio of carriages drew up and the civilians all boarded the rearmost one, the soldiers packing into the forward two carriages. Amy and I took seats across the aisle from Chambers and his family, the children excited to be aboard another train. It surprised me they did not pack the carriages to bursting with evacuees, but when I remarked upon this to Chambers, he merely shook his head sadly and would not be drawn further.

A whistle sounded, the carriage jerked into motion and we left the graves behind. As we headed West, we watched a column of thick, acrid smoke rising to the South over Guildford.

Chapter Seven

Evacuation

Among the handful of other civilians aboard the train were a couple of Chambers' colleagues from the Ares Project, although they could not provide us with much additional information about the state of the invasion. None of us was in any mood for small-talk, and we quickly fell into silence as we rattled through the countryside. At Basingstoke, the train was scheduled to stop at a pre-arranged spot outside the station to collect a few more men, but a crowd of people on the tracks forced it to a halt before this. They were asking for mercy, to be taken aboard and carried to safety — no doubt they knew, or at least believed we were on our way to some hidden refuge. Soldiers sprinted along the train to stand by each of the doors, rifles at the ready in case someone tried to force their way aboard. I thought I heard gunfire from the front carriage, and hoped I was mistaken. In any case, we were spared the sight of someone shot down in front of us. A few moments later, the train jerked into motion again amidst shouts and screams from outside. Despite myself, I could not draw my eyes from the window, watching the upturned faces of the people we passed as if searching for an old friend. I praised whatever good fortune had placed me on this side of the glass.

Amy pulled down the blind. "But we have space," she protested quietly, putting words to my discomfort. "Why could we not have taken a few aboard at least?"

Chambers shook his head. "If we had once opened the doors, they would have overwhelmed us. And whom would you choose? If we had space for half-a-dozen, or a dozen at most, how would you decide which of them we should take with us?"

"Why, we should save the women and children first, of course," I replied.

"Naturally," Chambers agreed. "But which women? Which children? Do you restrict each woman to choosing one of her children to bring along? Or does the washer-woman with five at her apron-strings outweigh three with a single offspring apiece?"

My voice caught in my throat. "So you choose none?"

"I have my orders," he replied sadly. "We have more stops to make, more people vital to our survival to collect. The world has changed. We shall have to become used to a new morality among many other things."

After this discussion I had little left to say to Chambers, and as our train rattled through the English countryside, I opened up the blinds again. Gazing out of the window at the scenery passing by, I would forgive you for thinking that nothing had changed at all. For most of the journey, everything appeared as if it was a typical autumnal day and we were off on an excursion. But from time to time, reminders of our fate hove into view.

Occasional pillars of smoke crested the horizon as we travelled onwards. I gave up trying to count how many after the first hour. Each bridge we travelled over crossed a road packed with people attempting to flee. A slow procession of humanity, seeking some refuge that I was sure they could never reach. Where would they go? Where might someone be safe? The Martians had landed all across the country — the world — and it was surely a fool's errand to seek sanctuary. I hoped that our own journey would have a happier destination than these.

We paused frequently to collect certain individuals and the odd small group of people, much as they had gathered us up at Brookwood. As we arrived at each halting point along the route, messengers boarded bearing telegrams for Chambers. With each new missive his mood darkened. By the time we reached the outskirts of Bristol, he was in a deep depression.

Shoving the telegrams over to me, he whispered "It seems we are lost," his first words since our disagreement. I took the papers and read of the progress of the Martians. The latest report was some few hours old, but even by that time some score of cylinders had already landed, and only two had been destroyed. There were no signs of fighting machines yet, which was a small if tangible relief, nor had the black smoke emerged. The columns rising through the air must have been fires started by the heat-rays, or perhaps by the impact of the cylinders. Reconnaissance had shown the Martians at work in their landing pits excavating rock and processing it, presumably to build their machines. I uttered a silent prayer for those brave men who had risked so much to bring us this news.

The death toll was rising fast, although no-one could make an accurate count. Whether most deaths at this point had resulted from the Martian heat-ray or the artillery is unclear; as the army learned of the rout of their colleagues elsewhere, many had fired on the cylinders before the civilians withdrew from the danger, perhaps hoping the shield the Martians employed might take time to establish. Riots and looting were widely reported, along with the columns of refugees I had seen crowding the roads. Each message I read increased my apprehension, my terror rising as note after note spelled out our utter inability to defend ourselves. Amy gently took the papers from me and returned them to Chambers, before grasping my shaking hands in her own, steadier ones.

At Bristol, we changed to another train. This one was longer, the extra carriages taken up with yet more soldiers. As we boarded, I heard a cacophony of shouts and screams coming from the station gates. They had, no doubt, boarded up the place for our safety, and the local populace was demanding entrance. I could not estimate the size of the crowd, but the volume alone suggested that it was at least a thousand strong. Hammering sounded at the gates, and I shuddered at the thought of them breaching the barriers. Reluctantly I accepted Chambers might had been right to refuse entry to a small number and risk being overrun.

Despite the larger train, we could not find seats. One gentleman offered his place to Amy, but she refused, wishing to remain by my side instead. The army had removed the seats from their own carriages, and crammed in like cattle, the press of their bodies the only thing holding them upright. We ourselves fared slightly better, being able to grasp the seat backs as we stood in the aisle. Amy passed me some bread and meat, and I ate mechanically. I had not realised that I was hungry until the food hit my lips.

Once under way we learned that we would not be stopping again until we reached our destination, "no matter the reason." I urged my fellow passengers to lower the blinds beside their seats, as I was sure the train would not even slow for a protest on the tracks.

I was feeling quite nauseated by the time of our arrival. The heat in the carriage caused by so many close-packed bodies was stifling, and the air took on a distinct scent of sweat and fear. I was glad to disembark and took deep breaths in the fresh countryside breeze that met me.

"Where are we?" I asked Chambers, when I located him in the crowd.

"Shropshire," he said. "The headquarters of the Ares Project. Or at least, the nearest station to it."

The station was larger than the one we had embarked at in Brookwood, though not by much. They crowded us into one corner of the area while the army gathered into formation and began marching up the road. With the crunching of their footsteps receding into the distance, I could hear birdsong for the first time in hours. Once again, it was startling how normal and mundane the world around seemed, even as our time on this planet might be coming to an end.

Chambers finished discussing something with one of the army officers who had met our train, and motioned all the civilians to follow him. He led us out of the station and towards a muddy field, churned by the wheels of the large diesel-powered lorries that stood arrayed across it. This was to be our transport,. Each lorry had benches along the two sides, and we scaled a short ladder to gain access to the rear. I went up first, and half-supported, half-lifted Amy in behind me. My nausea returned as we bounced along narrow and twisting country roads, clutching our meagre belongings on our laps. Peering out of the rear of the lorry, I saw the column of soldiers marching along, but also armed soldiers stood at readiness lining the route of our journey. I asked Chambers why.

"The government has declared Martial Law," he replied, shouting to be heard over the engine. "Looting has already started, the larger cities are paralysed by fear and rioting, and the rule of law has broken down."

"But we are far from the cities here," I pointed out. "Do you expect problems in this remote location?"

Chambers shrugged. "We had to secure the railway station. It might be over-cautious to prepare like this, but our Project's location and purpose was not exactly a secret among the local population. We believe they might feel safer close to us, when in fact almost all of all our operational defensive equipment is in the field already."

Amy's hand tightened on my leg, and I grasped it. "Might not the Martians attack you first?" Her voice was steady, despite the vibrations of the engine. "Are we in more danger here than we would have been at home?"

I attempted a tone of reassurance, which I told myself was for her benefit. "Not all the defences are gone, and at least here we will be far from riots and fighting."

"Moreover, we do not believe the Martians are aware of our importance," Chambers added. "Should that change, we have certain contingencies in place. I assure you, this is the safest place we can be at this moment."

The rest of the journey passed without comment, no-one keen to shout over the noise. I am sure also that each of us was still dealing with the events of the morning, and wondering what lay ahead. It must have been only about a quarter of an hour later when we arrived at the camp, although it felt longer. As we passed through the gates, I saw a small crowd being held at bay by armed soldiers, before the gates closed behind us.

Soldiers were to be seen everywhere, packing up equipment into tea chests and crates, loading it onto transports. They sprang into action loading our own conveyance with boxes as soon as we stepped out, and had left the camp before we'd even got our bearings. Chambers detailed a corporal with only one arm to show my wife and I to our accommodation, which he did grudgingly.

"I imagine you'd rather be out helping your fellows than showing us around," I suggested. He merely grunted and gestured to the pinned-up empty sleeve of his jacket. In my discomfort, I found myself asking how he had received his injury, and I was glad when he showed us our room and left without a word. Fortunately it was a private room, as I had feared (without mentioning to Amy, of course) that they might require us to share dormitory sleeping arrangements. The room was small and furnished only with two small, low beds and a battered wardrobe. Everything was a different shade of brown — from the walls to the bedspreads to the threadbare carpet and thin curtains — such a difference from the beautiful home we had fled. There was a shared bathroom along the hallway, and a common lounge area near the entrance to the building. Amy pressed against my side, and I extended my arm around her.

"I could not have brought enough to make this place pretty," she said. "But what I would give for a decent rug, or a painting on the wall at least."

"I am sure you will make this place as comfortable as anyone could," I assured her. "And that we are here together, and safe, is the most important thing to me."

She sat on the bed and patted the mattress for me to join her. "Sit with me a while," she said. "Let us catch our breath before we explore our new home."

I hesitated. "I was going to find Chambers," I began. Amy flopped backwards across the bed and let out a sigh. "I must know what is happening," I continued. "They brought me here for a reason, I have a duty to perform and a purpose to fulfil."

Amy sat upright again. "And what is my purpose to be? To wait here, stored like emergency rations until you have need of me again?"

"I am sure they will need assistance with something," I said. "I will ask on your behalf if you wish." She waved me away irritably. "And besides, I want to know of Frederick." A lump formed in my throat. "He was not on the train, but I hope he is here already, in safety."

Amy stood and crossed the room to embrace me. "Of course," she whispered. "But please, do not be long."

Chapter Eight

Refuge

I met the ill-tempered corporal who had shown us to our room outside the building and asked him where I might find Chambers. He directed me towards the canteen, and inside I found a small group of men in animated discussion, Chambers among them. The heated flow of conversation passed over him as if he were not there. He flashed me a watery smile when he saw me and pointed to a large teapot and collection of cups on a nearby table. I poured myself tea, helped myself to a stale biscuit, and waited for their discussion to end.

Before I was half-way down the cup, the group broke up and Chambers came over to see me.

"How are you settling in?" he asked. "No, how foolish, you've barely had time to look around. I shall ask my wife to look in on yours, they can get to know one another. I trust the rooms are to your satisfaction?"

"Quite," I replied. "Unless you have a stash of carpet or soft furnishings to share with us. But that is not why I am here."

"Right, to business then. No doubt you're keen to know your purpose here."

"I understood you wished my help with your war-games," I said. "Or have events overtaken us?"

"In a manner of speaking." Chambers replied. "You can still assist us as planned. But now that we are here that is no longer officially my purview, I'm afraid, and so I shall have to hand you over to another. Captain Russell should join us shortly."

He poured himself a cup of tea, but had no time to partake before a short man with a freshly pressed uniform crashed into the room.

"You must be the writer," he bellowed. I stood and introduced myself, but he ignored my outstretched hand. "I told Chambers and I'll tell you, I don't need another civilian gumming up the works here, let alone one who spills everything he discovers in the popular press."

His bluster left me at a loss for words for a moment, but I rallied. "I can assure you of my discretion in any and all matters which might affect the security of this nation. Indeed, my account in the 'popular press' was solely motivated by a desire to ready ourselves against the imminent return of our adversary." My lecturer's tones came back to me readily, and Russell appeared slightly abashed. Chambers' look of admiration made me uncomfortable until I realised that this meek man was jealous of my ability to put a bully in his place. "And besides, I suspect there will be no newspapers for some time, at any rate."

"What of your loyalties?" His question confused me. "Are you with us?"

"Who else would I be with?" I asked.

"I had to remove a few men who turned out to be of the more apocalyptic sort," he explained. "Thinking the return of the Martians was some sort of Judgement Day, or similar."

I thought back to the man at Speaker's Corner, the group at the sand pits, the curate. "I have no time for such nonsense. Humanity is the rightful occupant of this planet, and you have my word I share no sympathy for those creatures."

"Good," Russell continued. "But you're still a distraction. Prowling around asking awkward questions — I don't have time for it."

"Nor do you need to," Chambers said quietly. "I... I will be his liaison."

His arguments deflected, Russell had no retort but muttered under his breath something I couldn't quite catch. I would have my work cut out to convince him I was of any value.

"Speaking of liaison, what will be the manner of the war-games?" I asked.

At this, Russell butted in again. "Our *battle rehearsals* are no concern of yours. I really must draw the line there. Revealing our stratagems and tactics to an outsider would be most foolish." I looked to Chambers for some support, but found none. The three of us sat awkwardly in silence for a time before Russell stood. "Well, if that's all..." he said, and without waiting for a reply, stalked out of the room.

"Don't worry about him," Chambers assured me once the door was closed. "He's not in charge, despite his attitude. Or perhaps because of it. The Powers That Be approved your presence and involvement here, and he's just bent out of shape because they didn't consult him first."

So I was a visible reminder of Russell's lack of status. I resolved to keep out of his way whenever I was able.

Chambers continued. "Anyhow, before we begin any *battle rehearsals*," the sarcasm was clear in his voice, "it would be prudent to show you what toys you will play with."

As we walked, I raised the subject of my brother. "Is he here?" I asked.

Chambers shook his head. "He was destined for another location, and I'm afraid I do not know where. We have some communications channels available to us, so I will ask. He is a resourceful fellow, though, and I am sure he is safe."

I could only hope that he was correct. Thoughts flooded my mind as we walked. My brother was a key part of the government's planning and so would presumably join them in whatever stronghold they had. In light of his own experiences in the first invasion, I was confident he would have taken the threat seriously and not left his own evacuation to the last minute. Every rational thought I had reinforced the idea that he would be safe and sound, so why did I still fear for him?

On such deliberations, I passed the half-mile walk. Chambers had led me to the far end of the camp, and the rumble of machinery and squeaks of wheels had become audible as we drew closer. A high wooden wall surrounded the source of the sounds, preventing any observation.

"Russell is right about one thing, we do have some concerns about security," Chambers said, as he unlocked the entrance. Vast iron gates obscured with tarpaulins stitched together swung open and I took my first glimpse of our best defence against the Martians.

For the most part, technology advances by small increments, minor improvements to the existing state-of-the-art. Bicycles went from the Velocipede and Penny-Farthing to the safety bicycle with the application of gears and chains; old principles applied to new. But from time to time, we make a giant leap which appears to come from nowhere. The steam engine unlocked the power of coal and ushered in our current age, and resembled nothing that had come before it.

So it was with the device I saw now.

It was a full-sized version of the boxy model I had seen on the table in Chamber's London basement, but that child's toy could not have prepared me for the complexity of the contraption clanking its way around the churned up fields. It consisted of a large, flat box which must have been twenty feet long and ten wide. Along the sides of this many wheels were mounted, and on top sat a smaller box about half the size of the base. From this latter an enormous gun extended to the front, and what looked like twin barrels of machine guns on either side of that. Covered portholes ranged along the sides, above the wheels, from which I presumed it might deploy more guns. The overwhelming impression was one of strength and rigidity.

The wheels were joined by thick metal ribbons, arranged such that the machine laid its own road beneath itself as it lumbered forwards. Fountains of mud arced up behind it as it passed us, and clouds of dense black smoke emerged from a vent at the rear. The wind brought this toward us and I smelt the thick cloying scent of burning oil.

As I coughed, a target jerked into view on the far side of the fields. Unseen hands tugged a crude wagon covered in hay bales across the area on a rope. The top section of the machine turned to face it without the lower part stopping or changing direction, the gun sounded once and a cloud of white smoke engulfed the behemoth. A fountain of earth and then a ribbon of red smoke curled up a few feet ahead of the target, and a whistle sounded.

The smoke cleared to reveal a human figure peering from the top of the machine, oil-smeared and comically small against its bulk. He regarded the smoke critically and called down inside to someone.

"Too early, Jones, you need to lead it less." Seeing Chambers watching, he waved a greeting and clambered out and down the side of his steed. Stationary now, it still rumbled quietly like a sleeping beast.

"A beauty, isn't she?" he said as he offered a greasy hand for me to shake. I stood open-mouthed for a moment before absently taking it.

"What do you call that thing?" I asked.

He rolled and lit a cigarette with practised ease while we spoke. The acrid smoke from it was potent even above the smell of the machine. "Land Ironclad. Not as large as its naval namesake, but you get the idea. We have plans for larger ones, a hundred feet long..."

"Which we no longer have the time or resources to make," Chambers interrupted. "These should do nicely, though — they combine the mobility of cavalry with a sizeable fraction of the power of artillery. Once we get that gun to elevate reliably, we should be able to take pot-shots at any Martian fighting machine we see."

The Ironclad still enthralled me. "How do you operate it? What powers it? How fast can it go?"

Chambers laughed. "All in good time, let us allow Lawrence back to his practices." The captain of the Ironclad saluted, stubbed his cigarette out in a shower of sparks on the side of the beast, and clambered aboard. With a cacophony of grinding metal, the rumbling turned into a roar; it spun on the spot, the wheels and their tracks spinning in opposition to one another, and it rattled off towards the sheds that formed its home.

"That certainly looks to be a useful defence," I said when the sound diminished sufficiently to hear ourselves speak again. "The artillery pieces were sitting ducks — one shot each and then the Martians tracked them down."

Chambers nodded. "The Ironclads aren't too accurate if they fire on the move, but our crews are getting better. Even if they have to stop to fire, they can still high-tail it out before someone gets close. But they're not exactly stealthy, and their top speed lags that of the Martians."

"Do you have something in mind to address that?" I asked.

He hesitated just a moment. "Indeed, but that's still in the research stages and not ready to test just yet."

"Can you apply that remote operation you showed me to these Ironclads?" I asked, picturing the fellow Lawrence sitting at his ease while his fighting machine patrolled without him.

"In theory, yes. But we need line-of-sight for it to operate reliably, and in our testing, we often lost control. One rampaging Ironclad could cause as much damage as a Martian if it got loose. So for now we must risk the men inside."

"And what of the heat-ray? The armour might protect those men for a short while but they'd be baked alive in those metal boxes."

"We hope they will reflect a lot of the heat away, or absorb it harmlessly. We are only speculating though; without a working example of one to use ourselves, we cannot truly test our defences."

It startled me to hear this — surely the recreation of the Martians' most fearsome weapon would have been a priority. Chambers reminded me of the disasters at the laboratories, when attempts had been made to identify the science behind it. "Until we know more, it is simply too dangerous to attempt to modify it. It works by principles we do not understand and is extremely hazardous to life and limb."

I would discover the truth behind his words in time.

I joined Chambers in a map-room where instead of the relief map of Woking I had seen in London, there stood a vast map of the entire country. His peers immediately drew him into conversation, so I took a moment to regard the situation laid out before me.

I counted thirty of the cylinders, represented here by simple brass solids. I could detect no pattern to their distribution, other than it being fairly wide-ranging and encompassing most of the country. None was nearer to its neighbour than around fifty miles, in contrast to their first assault when all the arrivals had been within twenty miles of one another.

I learned of the destruction of the one nearest Edinburgh, and the brass cylinder placed there bore a miniature flag emblazoned with a skull and cross-bones. So too did one near Birmingham and one in Cornwall. As I waited, a young woman placed an additional cylinder on the edge of the map and used her long stick to push it over into Lincolnshire, coming to rest near Grantham.

Around each of the remaining cylinders were wood-carved field-guns, some lying on their side presumably to show the Martians had destroyed them. Others were being moved around along painted train tracks, destined for the battle. Wooden soldiers encircled each cylinder and were likewise being transported about, but there were precious few of them. Dozens of the tiny figures lay at the edges of the table, though whether they were awaiting deployment or had been removed from the field was unclear.

The model Ironclads numbered around a hundred — but stood further from the cylinders than the artillery. By now Chambers had finished his conference and I asked him about this.

"I see we deployed the Ironclads in time, but why so far from the Martians?"

"Their shells would not pierce the shields any better than the artillery, so we're holding them back. Once the fighting machines emerge, we'll be using the Ironclads as our primary weapon against them. We know that the artillery will have little chance of hitting a moving target. We trust the Martians will not be expecting a mobile attack force, nor one that can be hidden, so we might catch them by surprise — or the Martians themselves if they show their hides. Notice that we've encircled as many of the landing sites as we can, so whichever way the Martians go we ought be able to head them off."

"Do we have any information about the destroyed cylinders? Perhaps there is something that will give us insight into their plans?" I asked.

"They're larger than last time," Chambers said. "Much larger — but there's little enough we can find among the wreckage left by the explosive ordnance we used on them. It looks as though they brought more equipment with them, components for their fighting machines, perhaps. And there were more creatures inside than we saw previously."

A clattering noise at the rear of the room caught our attention then, and Chambers and I walked in that direction. A ticker-tape emerged from a telegraph, the dots and dashes of Morse code too quick for me to follow. When the tapping ceased, a woman collected the strip of paper, scanned them quickly and grabbed another cylinder from a box beside the table. Placing it on the map upon the left-most edge, she slid it with a well-practised grace directly over Shrewsbury, merely ten miles from where we stood.

Chapter Nine

Setback

I spent the rest of the evening in that place. With the latest cylinder practically on top of us, Russell was keen to complete the battle plan. He made no mention of his earlier protests against my taking part, so Chambers must have been right about his being overruled. I decided on discretion and did not rub my presence in his face.

The 'games' saw us split into two teams — one to play the role of the defenders, and another the invaders. The military contingent who would have a role in the field headed the defenders, so that they could try out their stratagems in safety. They assigned me to the side of the invaders, comprising a rag-tag bunch of junior officers barely old enough to be in long trousers.

"Should we not have," I struggled to think of a polite phrase, "a little more experience on our side? It will do no good if we are not a proper challenge."

Russell puffed out his chest. "I thought that was your purpose," he sneered. "If you are not up to the job, you can leave."

Russell granted us an hour to come up with battle tactics and contingencies, scarcely long enough for an amateur like me to make much of an impact. After his sniping at me, I could hardly complain, and resolved instead to make him eat his words before the end of the night. Each team retreated to a separate anteroom to plan, taking with them maps and notebooks for strategising.

"Right, chaps," I said as soon as the door closed behind us. "What I witnessed last time was..."

"Thank you, *sir*," one lieutenant said, stressing the honorific sarcastically. "But I believe we have the idea of it." The others sniggered quietly before huddling together around a table and ignoring me.

I watched and listened as they schemed, and had to admit they seemed well prepared. They knew the speed of the Martian fighting machines over varied terrain, the range of the heat-ray, how long it took the black smoke to fill an area, and a dozen other sundry facts and figures. What they lacked entirely, however, was any idea of what it all meant. To them, this was a purely theoretical exercise, a challenge to be overcome and nothing more. I saw a premonition of these young men in the field tomorrow, facing down a tripod as I had once done. At that moment, with that towering death-machine above me, I would not have been able to recall my name, let alone calculate the best method of countering an attack. I needed to prepare them for the reality of their situation.

They had by now formulated a plan and reluctantly agreed to explain it to me. I must have let out a snort, or a choked laugh at one point, because they all rounded on me.

"What is so funny?" one asked. I think his name was Wilkes.

"You've lined them up like infantry," I explained. "If you were facing Napoleon, that might work. But the artillery will make quick work of you all once they get the measure of your distance."

"So what would you have us do?" the youngest asked. He immediately withered under a glare from Wilkes.

"I watched them strike from all sides, spin about to come from behind. They come in one by one and get back out again just as fast. And they're quick, despite their size, so you must use that to your advantage. The Ironclads are slower, keep moving and they won't catch you."

As one, they turned to examine the plan they had drawn up. "A frontal assault makes the most sense," Wilkes explained. "Strike hard, overwhelm the lines and stride through."

"The most sense to you, perhaps," I replied. "And to the defenders. I'm telling you what I watched them do, and it was terrifyingly effective." I felt unclean, as if I was advising the Martians themselves, but I needed to remember that this benefited our side, and not theirs.

"Thank you, *sir*. I'll take it under advisement."

<hr />

The first battle lasted five minutes.

As I predicted, the defenders were ready for precisely that nature of assault. They had measured the distance to various landmarks and pre-aimed the artillery so that when the invaders appeared, they were quickly mowed down. The junior officers had lined up the tripods so close to one another that a single shell could do for two of them at once. The Ironclads were barely needed.

Wilkes stood staring at the board, the models of his fallen machines lying on their sides at the edges. He had managed little — only one artillery piece was ruled as 'damaged', and even I had to admit that it was more of a face-saving decision than an honest one.

As much as I wished that the coming war would be over so quickly, I knew it could not. If I had any purpose here whatsoever, it was to prepare these men, and if that meant crushing a few egos, so be it. Wilkes could hardly be more crushed than he already was.

"I did exactly what they taught us," he mumbled to himself. "Precisely what every lecture at Sandhurst told me to do."

"This is a new age, lieutenant," I said. "A new type of war. And that requires a new type of soldier."

"One like you?" I could hear an echo of Russell in his tone.

"Heavens no," I shuddered. "One who learns from his mistakes, and doesn't give up."

He turned to face me. "Look, we were told not to listen to you, that you were... well, never mind what he told us." Russell, I was sure. "But if I try your idea, what happens?"

I shrugged. "We see if it works, and then the rest of them can work out how to counter it. That's the point, after all."

"I mean, what happens to me?"

He looked terrified. What had Russell threatened these men with if they listened to me?

"Then you take the credit."

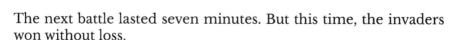

The next battle lasted seven minutes. But this time, the invaders won without loss.

I congratulated Wilkes on 'his' victory and loudly asked questions, playing the part of the dutiful chronicler trying to understand a military mastermind. Nevertheless I think my involvement was suspected. Chambers winked at me when no-one was looking, and some of the senior officers eyed me suspiciously.

Russell moved me over to the defender's side after that, certain that none of the senior men would listen to a mere writer. With an expectation of the attack pattern, the defenders were better prepared and made good use of their Ironclads to head off and ambush the invaders. The next battle was a narrow victory for the Martians, and after that, the defenders turned the tables on them more and more easily.

I couldn't shake the idea that things would never go this well, but knew that they would never heed my disagreement. Chambers, also sidelined, shared my concerns, so together we devised an approach that would at least give us something to do while the soldiers played at war.

"What if the Ironclads cannot engage?" I asked. "Once the Martians see how effective they are, I would imagine they'd avoid them at all costs."

"Then we use them to herd the enemy towards our artillery," Chambers replied, scrawling in a notebook.

"The artillery is hard to hide, they'd see it a mile off. What about sending men into the field with claymore mines and other explosives?"

"That's a good idea. But a man alone would be too vulnerable. Better to send a squad," Chambers said. "They could use steel cables to lay traps, trip them up."

"One man can hide where five or more would stand out," I argued. "And more easily be overlooked." I thought for a moment about hiding in the rubble of that fallen house, and how my companion at the time had almost doomed us both. "Alone, agile, and fast. That's the way."

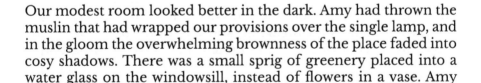

Our modest room looked better in the dark. Amy had thrown the muslin that had wrapped our provisions over the single lamp, and in the gloom the overwhelming brownness of the place faded into cosy shadows. There was a small sprig of greenery placed into a water glass on the windowsill, instead of flowers in a vase. Amy inquired immediately about my brother, and I explained what little I had learned.

"He will be fine," she assured me. "I know you believe that, even as you refuse to accept it. It's tiredness that makes you doubt him; we have had a very long and troubling day, and a good night's rest will cure all."

It was not to be. The beds were comfortable enough, if a little musty, and our tiredness drew us into sleep almost immediately, but a cacophony outside rudely awoke us in the early hours.

All day there had been a constant flow of men and equipment into and out of the camp, but now this had accelerated. A cylinder so near to our base of operations had caused considerable disruption, and the preparations would continue even at the cost of our own comforts.

When I eventually gave up on rest, I found I was not the only one awake early, as I was forced to queue for the shared bathroom facilities and consequently was one of the last to arrive for breakfast in the canteen. Fortunately, I found sufficient food laid out to feed a hundred more men, and so was not required to go hungry.

Sitting with Chambers and his peers, I set to work demolishing my bacon and sausage, while the men assembled there discussed the recent developments, having already finished their repast.

Overnight, we had established an observation post overlooking the crater in Shrewsbury, with a telegraph line established back to our 'war room'. The watchers there would relay any slightest movement in the pit back to us immediately, allowing a warning should the Martians move toward us.

Opinion was divided on whether they had planned the arrival for this location because of our camp's existence, to replace the destroyed cylinder at Birmingham, or whether it was merely one of the seemingly random landings designed to spread our defensive forces thin. In truth, it hardly mattered. We had a Martian on our doorstep.

Security at the gate had increased, as during the night a sizeable fraction of the residents had come to beg once more for sanctuary. All attempts to reason with them, to explain that if the Martians came this way, the camp would be a primary target rather than a safe-house, fell on deaf ears. Even now, we could still hear the chanting and calling from the gates over the noise of men eating.

Russell joined us for breakfast, and was all for breaking up the crowd by force if necessary, as he felt they were drawing undue attention to our location. "If the Martians see that lot, they'll be here like a shot," he said. "Send them packing and if they won't go, shoot a few! That'll scare the rest."

"We won't do that," Chambers said. "Our duty here is to protect mankind, not do the Martians' dirty work for them. They'll soon get hungry and go home, mark my words."

A messenger approached our table with a folded piece of paper in his hands. Chambers took it, and his face hardened. Russell snatched it from him and read it aloud.

"Three fighting machines seen in Wales. Black smoke used. Ironclads advancing."

His words were quiet, meant only for our table, but they galvanised the entire canteen into movement within moments. I bolted the last of my breakfast and followed Chambers' group to the war room.

I have referred to the heat-ray as the Martians' most fearsome weapon, and so it was. But the most deadly had been the black smoke. This it was that they had used to clear out resistance on their march to London. I recalled my close encounters with the thick, heavy vapour — and could not but wonder if my new acquaintances had made any progress in its understanding.

"We have begun to tease apart the mystery," Chambers explained as we walked, "but that is another area where the Martian understanding of science outpaces our own. No-one can understand how it kills so quickly, and needing such tiny quantities to do so — nor do we know why the Martians were so profligate with its use, when it is so deadly. Experiments have proven that the smoke kills by inhalation, not merely by touch, so a gas mask suffices to protect a man."

"And is it fatal also to the Martians?" I asked. "With artillery shells filled with that substance, perhaps we can end the fight before it begins!"

Chambers nodded. "We think so, inasmuch as our biology is similar." He saw my surprise and chuckled. "Superficially, we're very different, but they breathe the same air as us, take in water as we do. And as you witnessed, our bodies can nourish them and our bacteria can infect them. But we have had little success in replicating the smoke ourselves. There are elements present we do not recognise, and the chemistry besides is bafflingly complex."

"And what of those bacteria?" I asked. "The Martians would be foolish indeed to risk succumbing to them again. Might they leave us humans alone, believing us to be the source of their infection?"

"We can hope so," Chambers agreed. "But there are so many microbial forms on this earth, they will need to have found a protection against them. Since we do indeed see the invaders returning, we must assume that they have developed an immunity — either through inoculation or perhaps an anti-bacterial drug of some sort. If so, or even if they simply do not emerge from their machines to risk exposure, we must rely on our other means to stop them."

Atop the relief map, three small trilegged models stood at the Welsh coast, crude representations of the fighting machines I knew only too well. A rough-carved cloud painted black sat between them, over the town of Caernarfon. I prayed that the people there had kept their gas masks close to hand. As we entered the room, an additional tripod figure was pushed into place alongside these three.

"Where are they going?" Chambers asked. No reply came. "Are they moving at all?" he asked, to the same lack of response.

"Come on, people, we need information!" Russell barked. "Get on the damn telegraph and ask! While you're at it, ask the other stations for updates too, are they the only machines we see?"

"Is there any word from our nearby watching post?" I asked quietly.

"Nothing yet," the telegraph operator replied, before returning to his apparatus. I had hoped that it would take time for each cylinder to disgorge their occupants, but this arrival in Wales had been only yesterday — a few hours before our local visitor. If they'd already started the attack...

"Newcastle!" came a shout, and two more tripods were placed over that city. Within minutes, more sprouted over towns in Scotland and the North of England, and a few in the South. Guildford got its first machine shortly after that, and before long there were dozens of machines and almost as many clouds of black in all parts of the map.

"They must have been waiting," I guessed. "Lying in wait until all were ready before striking almost simultaneously."

Russell agreed, grudgingly. "We expected this. Obviously we hoped they would come out one by one, but that was never really likely." He glanced over at Chambers as he said this.

"It hardly matters," Chambers piped up. "All our Ironclads are in the field, and it's in their hands now."

For most of the morning, we had only reports from observer stations on the movement of tripods and the smoke, the map in front of us changing as the invasion unfolded. Major towns were the obvious targets of the Martians, who strode in with impunity, discharged their black smoke to quell any resistance and then moved on. None of the Ironclads could communicate directly with us given the range, and had to dispatch runners to telegraph sites or signal with semaphore to relay messages. The first report came in from Wales — at Caernarfon they could not engage the Martians effectively owing to the terrain. The mountains there made movement difficult for our Ironclads, but the three-legged fighting machines could bowl along at speed no matter the incline. A few shots had been taken, and while one gunner swore he'd hit a Martian dead-on, no evidence of damage was seen, and they deemed the account not to be trustworthy.

As the morning passed, more information came to us slowly. Many of the Ironclads were reported destroyed, and their corresponding models removed from the map table, but a good few had reported engagements with the enemy and survived to tell the tale. Wherever an Ironclad came up against a Martian, they fought bravely — guns firing rapidly and accurately — but to limited effect. Whether the shells were simply underpowered against the Martian armour or having to fire to such an elevation robbed them of their speed was a matter of much debate until a report came in from Shrewsbury.

Here the Ironclads to the Southeast of the town had advanced to higher ground. From there, their strikes were more direct when the fighting machines strode past and struck with greater energy. Rounds fired against them were clearly seen to bounce off the shell — or more accurately, from an invisible barrier a few inches away.

The tripods had shields as well.

Chapter Ten

Sighting

This discovery threw our plans into disarray. All of our war-gaming and strategies had assumed the fighting machines would resemble those seen before. Chambers informed me he had raised this concern during some of the early strategy sessions, but had been overruled.

"That's not true," Russell retorted. "You suggested them having better armour, thicker hulls. We all agreed that would limit mobility and agility, and would never occur to them. They barely saw us get a shot off last time, so why would they increase their protection?"

"The *Thunderchild* destroyed one," I reminded him, as Chambers bit his tongue. "And a couple of artillery pieces did some damage, too. That alone might have caused them concern."

"Perhaps," Russell said. "But you made no suggestion of shielding like this. And we don't have any weapon more powerful than the ones deployed, and so we'd have wasted time on circumstances we had no remedy for."

A general retreat was ordered — if the Ironclads could not pierce the protection afforded by the fighting machines, then they were not to be risked — and the crews sped away from the fields of battle. Unfortunately, the Martians most times hunted them down, evidently feeling that while the land ships were not a great threat to them, it would be better to be rid of their interference. I tried not to imagine the terror of the men trapped inside as the heat-ray hit, and hoped that their end was swift and painless.

Of course, bad news did not entirely dominate that day. While the cockpits of the Martian machines were indeed impregnable to our weapons, one lucky shot by a retreating Ironclad had crippled the leg of one tripod. At the speed the fighting machine was moving, the pilot had no time to compensate. When the time came for the injured leg to whip forward and take the weight of the machine, it was not able, and the entire contraption tipped over. The carapace hit the ground hard, a fountain of earth hiding it for a moment. When the dust settled, the Ironclad's crew observed smoke escaping from the metal shell and fired an additional round directly at it. The invisible shield did not stop this one, and it exploded deep inside the machine, to glorious effect.

We relayed this news immediately to all remaining machines, but striking the moving legs of a Martian proved almost impossible. Those crews who had the most success were on flat ground and able to predict with some accuracy where the leg was due to come down. With their shot already lined up, only a small adjustment was needed in the time available before the leg lifted again. Most gunners, no matter their talents, were hard-pushed to manage this delicate act in the time they had, and only a couple of tripods were felled. Still, it gave us hope.

At least until the first direct sighting of our local Martians came that afternoon.

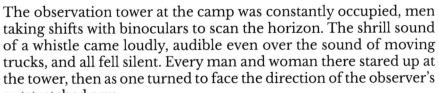

The observation tower at the camp was constantly occupied, men taking shifts with binoculars to scan the horizon. The shrill sound of a whistle came loudly, audible even over the sound of moving trucks, and all fell silent. Every man and woman there stared up at the tower, then as one turned to face the direction of the observer's outstretched arm.

Of course, we saw nothing. The Martian was too far to be visible from our elevation, but I sprinted up the tower steps and, panting for breath, arrived at the top in time to see the fighting machine.

It was at least a mile away and passed from left to right across my view. At that distance, it was impossible to make out details, but I could still tell that the main body was larger than the ones I had encountered before, and I believed the legs were a little shorter. I got the impression of greater strength, of sturdiness, and despaired at our prospects of defeating this new, more powerful foe. As I watched, Chambers arrived beside me, puffing even more loudly than I, and took the binoculars from the observer. He watched the machine in silence for a few moments before passing me the glasses.

I braced my arms against the rail of the observation tower, tried to still my breathing, and gazed out over the fields. The body of the Martian machine was definitely stockier than before — the joints reinforced and the carapace more angular than the ones with which I was familiar. No doubt whatever produced the shielding effect took up additional space inside, but I wondered whether there might also be more than a single Martian controlling it. The handling tentacles appeared thicker and stronger while hard at work, uprooting small trees and stacking them. The machine passed out of view behind a stand of trees, and I lowered the binoculars. My heart hammered in my chest, and I was not at all sure it was because of my rapid ascent of the tower.

"I wish we could just get our hands on one," Chambers sighed. With the tripod not approaching us, the panic was over for the time being. Perhaps they truly did not know of this camp's importance.

"Did you notice?" Chambers asked as we descended the staircase. "It didn't have any openings." He was right, I had seen none of the small vents or panels that were typical of the previous machines. "I suspect they're air-tight now, probably to protect them against bacteria."

"We expected that," I said. "We always believed that they would not come back unless they'd solved their problems with infection."

"Right, but might their chosen solution not present us with an opportunity?" he asked.

I did not understand what he meant, and told him so.

"If they cannot take in air from outside, then presumably they cannot take in water or food either. Since we know they need to eat, drink, and replenish their oxygen, they must return to a refuelling station or base at some point to achieve that purpose."

"The cylinders?" I suggested. "They also appeared larger than last time, you said."

He nodded. "They must have brought purification equipment, and if there are no vents in the machines, it suggests that it is not on board with them. Perhaps it is too heavy, or too power-hungry to carry about."

"But we cannot destroy the cylinders," I pointed out. "They are shielded as well as the tripods, if not better."

"Indeed, but those shields would no doubt prevent the fighting machines from entering as they would us — so they would have to remove them to replenish their supplies."

"We might have a chance," I agreed. "If an Ironclad can get a shot into the pit while the shields are inactive..."

Chambers called an immediate meeting to discuss the proposal.

It was infuriating to sit in a meeting while knowing the Martians stalked about unchecked, just miles from our location. Chambers was one of those types of men who one can only coerce into deciding when you have convinced him you have explored and exhausted every possible avenue. Russell, on the other hand, was as much a man of action as any I have ever known, keen to put any suggestion to the test at the earliest opportunity.

The clash of these two personalities in the small meeting-room led to a fractious discussion and I fear if I had not been present, then punches would have been thrown.

"It's on our doorstep," Russell pointed out, "just a mile away. Whatever else we plan, we need to protect ourselves. And if we can kill it, we should."

"And if we fail?" Chambers argued. "If we anger it, or tip our hand and reveal our location? We would invite a retaliation immediately which we could not repel."

"If it had looked over just then, it would have seen us. Sitting here will not keep us safe. Once that black smoke comes, once the red weed gets a grip, it will be too late. We must strike now."

I understood Chambers' caution, but I also agreed with Russell's assessment. Time was of the essence, with machines on the march all over the nation. If we could find a weakness and exploit it, then we might turn the tide of this war almost before it began. I threw my support to Russell, and eventually we convinced Chambers to allow an attempt at destroying the nearest cylinder. He asked Russell to allow me to join him as he made the preparations. Russell scoffed at this, but I ignored him.

"If this is to be the turning point in the conflict, as you so clearly believe it is," Chambers said, "We shall need our foremost Martian chronicler to be in attendance."

I demurred at his flattery, but was secretly pleased to witness the assault. He assured me we would be at a safe distance.

Russell reluctantly told me to follow him and strode towards the canteen. Inside, he canvassed the soldiers currently at their dinner for volunteers — practically every hand in the mess went up instantly. He selected a Sergeant and asked him to prepare a small team of six men to travel the following morning. As Russell and I left the room, volunteers pitching their suitability surrounded the Sergeant. It fairly warmed my heart to see the enthusiasm for the fight.

Amy was less enthusiastic about the idea, and her reticence only grew when she learned I planned to accompany this effort.

"No." She spoke flatly, wishing to prevent any argument. "You are no soldier, and your place is here with me."

"I can report the battle," I argued. "Bear witness to our first true strike against this foe."

"You have a wonderful way with words," she agreed, "but you can work that magic just as well with a second-hand report as you can with your own observations. Why would you want to place yourself back in harm's way when we have a sanctuary here?" She gestured around herself at our modest accommodation. She had found some candles which guttered on a low table, and had scavenged a threadbare rug from somewhere.

"I need to see it," I said. "It will finally put to rest that lingering fear, I know it. It will allow me to close that chapter of my life once and for all."

"And what did you feel when you watched the war machine striding across the horizon? Be honest, what emotions did it stir in you?"

I did not need to stop and think. "Fear, of course. It would be foolish not to be afraid. And dread, a vile apprehension at the sight of them once again. But mostly anger."

"I have that too; how dare they return, how dare they threaten us once again? But unlike you, I accept it is not my duty to run towards them. I have no obligation to dash myself to pieces against them to salve my conscience. Stay here, stay safe, and stay with me."

Had I truly been allowing my emotions to rule me? I examined my feelings and appreciated that she might be correct. What had I actually achieved since we had arrived here? I had defused a couple of arguments between Chambers and Russell at most. I had to concede that the feeling of uselessness that engendered was clouding my judgement. On the other hand, they had granted this sanctuary for a reason, and I was compelled to show that there had been justification in extending the offer to Amy and me. But they had never made mention of my taking part in military operations, so even Russell could not complain if I refused to accompany him. Indeed, it would please him not to have 'that accursed writer' following him around.

"You're right," I conceded. "My desire to see vengeance wreaked out against them should not encourage me into the field. I will let Chambers and Russell know at first light."

Amy embraced me, and we slept deeply until my alarm woke me before dawn.

Amy stirred as I dressed, and I planted a gentle kiss on her forehead before tiptoeing out. I would make my way to the map room, explain the decision to Chambers and Russell, and then return to spend the day with Amy. The sun had not yet risen, and even the birds had yet to start their morning chorus as I crossed the site.

However, on arrival, I discovered some sobering news. Our command post had been in contact with the government in exile since the beginning of the crisis, the cabinet and key ministers being evacuated from the capital as soon as the Martians had launched. Their exact location was unknown to us, but believed to be a quarry somewhere in Wiltshire. At some point overnight, the connection had broken, whether because of the severing of the telegraph lines or something more sinister was as yet unknown, but the radio operator could raise no one either.

"Our last communication was yesterday evening," Chambers informed me. "And included the news that your brother Frederick was indeed there, safe and sound." I breathed out a vast sigh of relief. "There may be an innocent explanation for the loss of contact. A search party is en route, but won't get there until mid-morning," Chambers said. "We can't wait for their go-ahead so the mission is proceeding as planned."

I took a deep breath to explain my decision of the previous night and found myself unable to speak. If the government were at the location in Wiltshire, it would be heavily guarded and all but impregnable. There could be nowhere safer for my brother to be. But losing communication had me worried. It suggested that they were vulnerable after all and rendered our mission even more important. If we could make a difference here, then all of our soldiers around the nation could learn from us, and keep everyone safer. My reunion with my brother could come sooner, and so would our return to normality. I felt obliged to do this for him, and for everyone.

In that instant I decided. I would go. Russell asked what my wife's opinion had been, and I muttered something non-committal about not wanting to wake her.

Russell and I met up with Sergeant Webb and his compact unit of volunteers who were champing at the bit to face the Martians. After a quick review of the map, we set off on foot, all the transport vehicles being occupied. The crowd who had taken up residence at the gates was smaller now, but clamoured around us as we left, begging to be let in. Russell barked at them and ordered our escort to ready their rifles as a warning; they backed away cautiously and let us through.

We had around ten miles to cover and the military folks set a lively pace. It was a chilly morning, and I'd wrapped up warm against the frost, but now I needed to strip off an outer layer as my exertions had warmed me considerably. My cycling and hiking practices stood me in good stead and I was just able to keep up. I let Russell do most of the talking, preserving my breath to not appear winded. He speculated on how large an explosion we could expect, and informed me he had been doing some calculations to ensure that we would be a safe distance from any effects. That the mission might fail had clearly not occurred to him at all.

After two hours, the sun was poking above the horizon, and we stopped for some very welcome refreshment. We drank tea brewed over a small 'Tommy Stove' and ate bully beef and bread. Our bellies filled, if not entirely satisfied, we moved on to the rendezvous location marked on our map.

We arrived to find an Ironclad already waiting for us, the name 'William Kite' painted on the side of its turret. To my surprise, I saw Lawrence leaning on the vehicle's tracks, surrounded by his habitual cloud of cigarette smoke. He offered us tea he'd brewed with the heat of the Ironclad's engine, and it was considerably warmer and tastier than the cup we had drunk earlier.

"You named your Ironclad?" I enquired. "I suppose we name their sea-going cousins."

He exhaled a fetid cloud of cigarette smoke, and nodded. "For an old friend," he explained in a tone that suggested no further questions would be answered.

"The cylinder is about three quarters of a mile away, in that direction," he told us, gesturing over a small rise in the land. "The fighting machine went off yesterday and we haven't seen it since."

"I ran some calculations," Russell said, "estimated their oxygen and food usage. It'll be back later today. Get your men into position, but you stay here Lawrence. I have some matters to discuss."

Lawrence nodded, gave some orders to the men inside the *Kite*, and banged on the side. A few moments later, it rumbled into life again. Clattering its way over the rise, it was far from stealthy, and as we followed I scanned the horizon for signs of the tripod returning. Russell and Lawrence brought up the rear, deep in discussions I would have loved to have overheard. However, I didn't want to anger Russell, who seemed to have warmed to me slightly since setting out. Perhaps he saw my silence as a sign of agreement with his nattering, rather than the shortness of breath it truly was.

Fortunately, no Martian appeared to threaten our advance. We found a suitable location approximately a quarter-mile from the cylinder on elevated ground, giving us a clear view into the pit through our binoculars. They had propped the cylinder upon its end, one circular face beneath the earth and one aimed skywards. Once the Ironclad was in position, Sergeant Webb's team set to work cutting branches and bracken to hide the metal beast from view, and within a short while the only hint of our presence was the stubby barrel of the weapon protruding from a thicket of greenery and the gentle wisps of steam from our breath. I tried to muffle my breathing as if the Martians might overhear me.

We settled in for a long wait, taking turns to watch the cylinder for any evidence of Martian activity. Had they deserted the site completely, or left one or more of their number to hold the location against attack? Perhaps they trusted their shields to protect the equipment within.

A brave volunteer, Private Cooper, headed down the hill to get a closer look and assist us in our attack. When he was in position, hidden a hundred yards from the pit, he signalled us with a heliograph and we all held our breaths.

Chapter Eleven

Striking

L ying in the chilly morning air, I was glad I had bundled up again. My fingers grew chilled, and I clenched and unclenched my fists as rapidly as I could to force some life back into them. My face was numb and the frigid earth beneath me sapped the heat from my belly. I pushed bracken beneath me to act as a mattress, earning me a petulant 'hush!' from Russell. Now lightly insulated, I settled in for an interminable wait.

At a little after ten o'clock, Sergeant Webb let out a low whistle. He pointed to the horizon to our right, and we watched the unmistakable silhouette of a Martian tripod rising above the trees. A hurried check of our equipment confirmed we were ready for action, and we lay deathly still as it passed a terrifyingly short distance from us.

It stopped at the edge of the pit where the cylinder lay and stood immobile for a few moments. The gun of our Ironclad was already aimed at the cylinder, but now we faced a tough choice — should we instead aim to destroy the fighting machine? We had little time to ponder, and in fact, the Martians made the decision for us.

The tripod stepped down into the pit. Despite the reduced elevation, it still towered over the landscape, but within moments we realised the legs were telescoping shorter, and the carapace was descending slowly towards the cylinder beneath. The surface of the lower structure opened in readiness to meet it, the entire top face opening like an iris revealing gloom within.

"Wait for it..." Russell whispered, his voice startling us as we lay hidden. With a clang audible even from our position, the tripod came into contact with the cylinder. Vents of steam or compressed air gushed forth from the interface between the two machines.

"Now! Fire!" Russell bellowed, and an instant later, the ground beneath me shook as the mighty Ironclad's gun fired. My ears rang, and the surrounding scene blurred. I shook my head to clear it and then looked back at our adversary just in time to see the effects of the round's impact.

A fountain of earth flew up, the shock of the explosion reaching us a moment later. When the dust settled, we could see the tripod still squatting undamaged in the pit. A sequence of flashing lights from Cooper's heliograph informed the gunner he had missed long, and a second shot followed in short order.

This time, the explosion was much greater. A blinding flash preceded a deafening boom that shook the earth once more, and debris from the destroyed tripod rained down over a wide area. Clods of earth came down just in front of us, and I feared that rocks or metal shrapnel might impale one of us. As the smoke cleared, revealing tangled wreckage in the pit, a cheer rose from the men, though I could barely hear it over the ringing in my ears. The jubilation ended abruptly as Webb saw through his field-glass that Cooper was trapped beneath a large metal plate, and not moving.

Heedless of whether the Martian was still a threat to us or not, we set off at a run to the poor man's aid. When we arrived, he was already dead. With all hands gathered, we lifted his tomb from him and carried his body carefully back to the *Kite* for transport to the base, and a hero's funeral.

<hr/>

Before we could deal with our loss, however, we had to investigate our prize. This was the first of the new fighting machines our group could examine at close range.

To Russell's chagrin, the damage caused by the round left very little of the machine to explore, but the tripod's bulk had protected the cylinder beneath from too much injury. The shell was still open at the top, where it had mated to the tripod, and cables and pipelines disquietingly reminiscent of viscera and entrails stretched between them, leaking fluids. Russell was eager to get inside.

"The Martians will know of this already, they'll be in communication and will come and investigate. The nearest machine is about an hour away, so we need to act fast." He issued orders, telling Webb to post lookouts and prepare to lower him in on a rope.

Sergeant Webb threw a grappling hook upwards, and after a few attempts fell short, one caught and held. Webb hauled himself upward, hand over hand, along the rope, and reached the top of the structure in a few moments. He straddled the edge, found his footing inside, and motioned for us to follow.

Russell insisted on going first, naturally, and we stifled our chuckles as he struggled to ascend. He had a grasp of the theory of rope-climbing, that much was clear, but little practice. His feet braced against the side of the cylinder kept slipping, and at one point I gasped as his hands slithered down the rope and I feared he would fall. Doubtless fuelled by the adrenaline this mishap had caused, he made it to the top and secured a rope to lower inside. He then donned his gas mask as protection against any Martian bacteria before rappelling inside and out of sight.

He was inside the machine for only a few minutes before he called for help. I was the only man not otherwise engaged in defensive duties, so it was my turn to ascend. I knew my limitations, and Webb lowered a rope down for me to tie around myself, and with his assistance bearing some of my weight, I could climb up with difficulty. Once on the rim, I peered inside but could see nothing in the dark interior of the cylinder.

"Hurry up," Russell called out, and once I had put on my mask Webb unceremoniously lowered me into the cavern by a rope around my waist. It dug into my skin and made my breathing even harder than the mask did, but all thoughts of discomfort vanished when my eyes adjusted to the gloom and I beheld the inside of an interplanetary craft for the first time.

The sight utterly perplexed me, unable to identify any point of reference by which I might orient myself or understand the craft's operation. The dim light did not aid this task, and Russell's hand-held torch provided merely infrequent flashes of illumination as he waved it about. Only when I ignored the current direction of gravity and considered the craft in its intended operation in space, could I make sense of it.

For the sake of my description, let us assume that the end of the projectile buried in the earth formed the front of it as it travelled. We had therefore entered through the rear. The curving walls as we perceived them now would have been horizontal during the craft's flight, though with no gravity acting upon the vehicle or its occupants every inch of their surface could be given over to equipment and apparatus without regard for somewhere to step or sit. Nothing I saw was recognisable to me, even the controls were unusual.

My feet reached the ground, and the rope slackened slightly, allowing me to walk around. The walls were a rust-red colour, though not from corrosion. Perhaps the occupants had painted it to match the dominant hue of their home world, or perhaps their eyes operated on different frequencies of light and they perceived glorious artworks where I saw merely reddish-brown.

I can not describe the cylinder as comfortable, at least not to my own sensibilities. I had to cast aside any thoughts I might have had of padded chairs to cushion a fragile body against the violence of launch and landing. How they might protect themselves during those times was merely one of a myriad of questions to which I had no answer.

Deep recesses burrowed into every available surface. I peered into one as best I could through the gas mask and saw a multitude of buttons and levers inside. Each of the holes must have contained dozens of such controls, presumably designed for operation by tentacles rather than fingers. I resisted the temptation to poke and prod inside one, partially to avoid triggering some unknown function, but mostly out of an irrational fear it might bite down on my hand and devour it.

The front of the cylinder housed large windows, now black as the craft's landing had buried them beneath the earth. No, when Russell's torch-light hit them, they didn't show soil, but remained black. I realised they were the displays on which pictures akin to those I'd seen in the lab would be projected. In front of them were multitudinous buttons, dials and levers whose function could only be to control the craft's operations. Russell himself was now occupied in the centre of the space, having hauled himself up the various outcroppings on the cylinder's side like a mountain climber. I clambered up and joined him in examining a large square metal apparatus to which most of the pipes which had passed between the cylinder and the tripod attached.

"Hold the torch," he ordered me, and I obliged. "See here, this lever must control the air-flow — now it's set to push it through the pipes, but if I pull on it..." Before I could object, he tugged a large oddly curved lever towards himself. With a loud clunk, it slid forward and a gentle breeze emanated from the equipment. It carried a pale greenish smoke along with it.

"Put it back," I urged him, trying to back away. With the torch in one hand, I could not climb down. "It might be toxic."

He scoffed. "Trust your mask, man. I need a sample." He busied himself with collecting some of the airflow into a syringe by inserting it into the vent. I tried not to breathe too deeply. My heart pounded in my ears and the very walls seemed to close in on me, an impression not helped by the flickering shadows cast by Russell's movements. I was sure I saw a tentacle writhing up beside me and spun the torch to see. Nothing was there, but my panic did not subside.

"Hold the light steady!" Russell barked. Eventually, he corked the syringe and returned the lever to the original position, and I let out my breath. He then set to work removing the entire apparatus from the wall. The Martians appeared not to employ screws or similar fixing methods, preferring instead a type of glue which supported and secured their items while allowing them to be removed and relocated easily. A few moments of work with a crowbar from his backpack saw the air generator removed, and the wires and pipelines leading out of it cut through with a large, highly polished knife from his belt. Russell's cavalier approach, with no heed for his own safety, alarmed me — had a large voltage been present in those wires, it could have killed him. He untied the rope from his waist, attached it to the lever on the top of the device, and called up to Webb to lift it out. As it slowly ascended, spinning on the end of the rope, a call came back down to us.

"Martian!"

We had been inside for barely half an hour and had expected no reprisal for our attack so soon. Russell allowed me to ascend before him, for which I was grateful. If he had not, I might have climbed the walls despite the risk of falling. Even so, he would only let me go after the air generator was lifted to safety. As they pulled me upwards in the improvised sling, I squinted up into the brightness and asked how far the Martian was from us.

"Still a mile, but he's coming fast," Webb called down. "The *Kite* is preparing to cover us, but we should get going."

I reached the top and clambered out, hands already untying the rope from my waist to throw it back down to Russell. The Ironclad was trundling noisily towards the North, and I thought I saw the vague outline of a fighting machine in the distance through the cloud of dense oily smoke the gun platform emitted.

"How long?" I asked, tearing off my mask and gasping for breath.

"Get going," Webb urged, ordering three of his men to accompany me. Two of them bore the captured device between them, using a jacket as a sling. Webb and the last of his team stayed to pull Russell up as we dashed for cover.

We had barely covered any distance before we heard the Ironclad's gun firing, and turned to look. The Martian was close, but the gunner's aim was good. An explosion against the side of the Martian's carapace staggered it, almost knocking it off-balance for a moment, and we dared to hope it might fall. It righted itself, turned to face the source of the attack, and the heat-ray came to life.

The undergrowth around the Ironclad flashed into flame instantly, burning so hot that it barely smoked. The vehicle tried to reverse out of the path of destruction, but the Martian held the heat-ray on it no matter its gyrations. Lawrence uttered a quiet prayer for his colleagues, and I willed my eyes to close, unable to watch those brave souls meeting their doom. Some macabre impulse led to me reopen them a moment later, just in time to see the barrel of the gun hanging limp and melting, the turret glowing cherry-red. Then a sun-bright flash, followed by a dull thump and a wave of heat reached us, and I knew the *William Kite* was no more. The magazine had exploded, and I prayed that the men inside had not felt the full heat of that dreadful weapon before their end.

While we stood there dumbfounded, Russell, Webb and the rest caught up with us and shook us out of our stupor. "Come on," Russell urged, "we have to get this thing back to base," and dashed off toward our camp. We roused ourselves and followed, casting glances over our shoulders in case the fighting machine should follow.

Chapter Twelve

Confrontation

W e made our way through the wooded area at the best speed we could manage, hopeful that the Martian could not spot us through the forest canopy. Every crack of a twig or rustle of leaves made my heart leap in my chest. When the woods thinned out and we needed to cross open grassland, our nerve faltered. I peered behind us, half-expecting to feel the flash of the heat-ray or smell a cloud of the black smoke billowing towards us.

The Martian stalked about over his fallen comrades, a mile or so behind. We caught our breath and discussion started as to the best approach to take. Some men were in favour of running for it, which Russell quickly put a stop to.

"Their vision systems have a decent range, from our experiments — if we can see it, it can see us. Running will draw its attention, and its fire. We might make it to safety if we're cautious."

Ultimately, we agreed to split up; we'd move in small groups and spread out to appear unthreatening and hopefully uninteresting to the Martian. Russell went ahead with the two privates carrying his prize, to monitor it and oversee its safe return. He threw his own jacket over it to hide it from sight, in case the Martian should recognise it as stolen property.

The three men set off at a gentle walking pace that, to my eyes, appeared more suspicious than a sprint would have been. As they covered the open terrain, the rest of us laid low and watched the Martian. Its head moved from side to side, scanning the surrounding area, and we held our breaths each time its gaze came in our direction. At any moment, we were ready to shout a warning, to urge our colleagues to run or hide, but the tripod seemed content to guard its location and not investigate a handful of men in the countryside. We hoped that its destruction of the

Ironclad *Kite* and the deaths of the men within had satisfied it to the elimination of any danger.

After the trio passed out of sight, Webb and I set off along the edge of the forest with the last of the men. We emerged from the cover of the woods about a half-mile away from where Russell and his porters had done, and forced ourselves into a slow, casual walk as best we could. Nevertheless, we glanced over our shoulders from time to time to see if the Martian was pursuing us. My feet kept trying to speed up, to break into a jog or a run, and it took every ounce of willpower I had to keep to a walking pace.

Our hearts leapt to our mouths at least twice as the machine changed position — once coming a few hundred yards in our direction before stopping again and resuming its surveillance. What purpose it might serve was unclear to us. Perhaps it was searching for an additional threat, or maybe just awaiting orders, but we were glad when we opened enough distance to see it vanish below the horizon.

We met up again with the rest of our company around a mile from the camp. Sergeant Webb ordered a much-needed rest and handed out such refreshments as remained. The men who had been carrying the air generator were exhausted. It was relatively small, about the size of a bread-box, but it weighed a good deal more than the size suggested. Two of the soldiers who had accompanied me took over the porterage duties, and we resumed our trek to our erstwhile home.

Before we got to the gates, we noticed the crowd of residents had grown, and Webb stopped us short before they caught sight of us. Their distant chanting of 'let us in' carried over to us.

"If we go up there, they'll overwhelm us," Webb said as we took cover behind a farm outbuilding. "We'll never get in without them storming the gates."

"Nonsense," Russell replied, "you and your men will clear us a path and we'll march right in." He moved as if to leave, and I placed a hand on his arm to pause him.

"Sergeant Webb is right," I said. "I have learned what happens when men are terrified, and heard my brother's reports of the exodus from London during the last invasion. These people are desperate, and will not hesitate to use our arrival to force their way in."

Russell scoffed, and I saw he was not to be dissuaded. Webb and I exchanged a glance, and then he nodded almost imperceptibly at me.

"Very well," I conceded. "But let me do the talking, and no-one is to shoot anyone."

We must have made a strange sight, marching slowly up the main road line abreast, two of our number carrying something on a sling between them. At Webb's suggestion, the men held their rifles ready, though at my request they all ensured the barrels pointed down and away from the crowd.

A man at the rear of the gathering caught sight of us first and hailed his fellows. Within moments, the entire mass turned and swarmed towards us, their chanting stopped. I froze, and the soldiers formed a line in front of me, taking a knee and moving their guns to be visible, though still not aimed at anyone. At this sight, the vanguard of the crowd slowed, and came to a halt about a stone's throw from us.

Conscious of everyone's eyes on me, I held up a hand for silence and waited until the murmuring died away. It was up to me now.

"Gentlemen!" I called, my voice pitched to carry to the back of the audience. "And ladies," I added, seeing a few in the assembly. "We come bearing intelligence to use against the Martians, and we must be allowed to pass." Silence greeted my words for a moment before one man pushed to the front and addressed me.

"And we must be allowed safe shelter," he said. "Your camp can take us all in, and you're the ones that have brought the Martians down on our heads. Let us in!" A cheer met his words, and the chant of 'Let us in' began over. I raised my hand again, unable to make my point over their noise.

This time silence was longer in coming. "We did not bring the Martians, in fact, we have just destroyed one! And we can continue to do so if you just allow us to pass." To my alarm, they met this with boos.

"I bet you have," their spokesman jeered, "that's why you've got to let us in! You think they're just going to let that slide? They'll come here and wipe us out just for sport! And your damn land-ships are no use neither, we know that. You won't protect us, you're just locked up in there, safe as you like, and don't give a God-damned cuss about the rest of us!" The crowd cheered him again and surged forward a few feet.

The soldiers snapped their rifles to their shoulders in a split second, and the oily click of the bolts being slid into position silenced the crowd more effectively than my upraised hand could have. Time was running out to avoid a catastrophe.

"We are defending all of you, all the nation, just the best we can," I started, but jeering drowned out the rest of my words.

"This is pointless," Russell murmured in my ear. "Shoot the ringleader, the rest will scatter," he said to Webb.

"No!" I called out, though Webb showed no inclination to pass on the order. I addressed the crowd again. "We have a duty to do; we can win this fight but we need to go back inside. We have seen no sign that the Martians know of this place, and have seen no reprisals. The nearest one is over Shrewsbury and poses no threat to you at all. Go home!" I felt my exaggeration was justified in the circumstances. If they knew one was as close as it was, any chance we had of resolving this peacefully would evaporate. A few of the crowd looked like they might have listened, but the pressure of their peers kept them in place.

"Or we will open fire!" Russell shouted, a crack in his voice reducing the impact his words might have had. At this, more of the assembled locals shifted uneasily, but still no-one left. The men's rifles never wavered, but a couple of them glanced up at me with pleading in their eyes, and I knew they would never fire on the civilians.

I noted Russell gazing over the heads of the crowd blocking our way and followed his eye-line. There was a man I vaguely recognised standing in a watchtower beside the gate. He made some quick gestures with his arms, like a semaphore signaller, and waited for a reply. I looked around to see who he might be signalling, but no-one was there apart from our little band.

Russell had clearly been the intended recipient of his message, and he turned on the spot, his eyes scanning the horizon behind us. He gasped, and I looked to see the unmistakable outline of a Martian fighting machine appearing over the horizon. I prayed the crowd would not see it, but in vain. Within moments cries and shouts broke out, and they looked ready to flee. Their spokesman stood up straight and appealed for calm, which came slowly.

He addressed me directly. "You said they were not here, and yet here they are. You said that they would not avenge their fallen brother, and yet here they are. You must now let us in and protect us!"

He strode towards me, the line of rifles not bothering him in the least. As he reached them, our guard stood and blocked his path, but the rest of the crowd surged forward and threatened to surround us. I attempted to stand my ground, but Webb pulled me aside and led a retreat, the rest of our group following with their rifles still trained on the crowd.

All of our group except for Russell, who stood to one side and made his own series of windmilling gestures. I did not know what they might signify, but they were evidently understood by the man in the watchtower as he snapped a salute and disappeared. Russell gazed after him for a moment and then joined me.

"Come on, we need to get out of here," he urged me, and led us all back to the farm building we'd sheltered behind before. The mob at the gates didn't follow us, whether they believed they had repelled us or merely didn't want to approach the Martian any closer, I wasn't sure, but I appreciated not being trapped among that mass of humanity.

Then the screaming began.

Chapter Thirteen

Massacre

Somehow, hearing the panic at the gates was worse than witnessing it. The mind fills in the gaps with the most horrifying images at its disposal, and mine had more than its fair share of those.

Gunfire rattled — warning shots, I hoped — which precipitated the first of the screams. The sound of a crowd in panicked flight is something with which I am all too familiar, but I had to admit that anything less than a direct threat would have moved that group. I was glad it had not fallen to me to order it.

Dozens of the protesters fled down the road, which took them past our hiding spot, before they realised they were sprinting towards the distant Martian and changed direction. As the terrified screams of the scattering mass filled our ears, the shrubs just a few feet away flashed into flame. I looked up at the distant Martian — surely it was too far away to use the heat-ray? Indeed, it was so far away that it wasn't even clear whether it was looking in our direction. But if not from that machine, from where had the attack come?

With a sickening certainty, I realised it was not from any Martian, but had to have come from inside our own base. I looked into the faces of my companions and saw only horror staring back at me. Russell had been so keen to get us to safety after his signalling, he must have had something to do with it. But when I looked in his direction, Russell appeared as shocked and nauseated as the rest of us, and that forced me to reconsider my hasty opinion. When I asked him what he had intended his frantic signalling to do, he merely shook his head, tight-lipped and pale.

It seemed an eternity until the screams stopped, though it was probably only a few seconds. The sounds of panic and terror ceased, leaving only the bangs and crackle of burning undergrowth, and the heaving vomiting of a soldier.

"Come on," Russell croaked, and stepped out from behind the building. Dazed, I followed him.

We stepped out into a scorched hell. Within a distance of two hundred yards from the gates, everything in sight was black and smoking, even the asphalt on the road bubbling and flowing down the gentle hill. Of the crowd once gathered at the gate, only a few were still visible in the distance, fleeing as if the devil himself pursued them. I prayed they had all made it out of range before this atrocity had begun.

Charcoal cracked under our feet as we stepped on what had once been grass. One private stumbled onto the road and his boots began to smoulder — the quick thinking Webb pulled him back to safety and doused them with water from his canteen.

As we approached the gate, I realised that not all the poor unfortunates had reached safety. A handful of men had been inside its effective range and were now charred beyond recognition. Soldiers from inside were now engaged in breaking their carbonised bones free of the metal gate and they crumbled into powder. The heat rising from the ground lofted the ashes to scatter in the afternoon wind. I was glad that wind was behind us, sparing us from inhaling the remains of our fellows. I heard vomiting behind me once more, and fought to control the bile rising in my own throat. My nerves were so highly-strung that each crackle of the fires the heat-ray had started echoed in my head like gunshots, and I flinched every time.

Guards directed us around the perimeter of the camp and we made our entrance through a side-gate. This positioned us behind one of two turrets that overlooked the entrance. I had always assumed they were machine-gun posts for our defence, but now I saw that this one at least contained a larger threat. Emerging from the top of the tower, still glowing red from the heat it had disgorged, was a large version of the Martian heat-ray projectors. The cavity within was making metallic clanging sounds as it cooled, and something about the pitch of the sound set my teeth on edge.

Russell had shaken off his disquiet and begun ordering men about, the air-box we had rescued being loaded into a truck to be taken somewhere, but I paid him no heed. I needed to speak to Chambers. Surely he could never have resorted to such a measure?

I found him in the map-room, updating the locations of our forces. Angrily I recounted to him the atrocity I had witnessed, and it frightened me when he didn't appear shocked, but he led me away to a quieter room to discuss it.

"You knew of this?" I barked as he closed the door behind us. "You knew?"

He kept his voice measured, almost cold. "I knew we had a heat-ray, yes. But you have to believe me: I did not know that it was operational."

"You told me we couldn't use it!" I cried.

"I said that it was a danger, that we didn't understand it, and that it posed an extreme hazard to life and limb. All of this was, indeed is, true. But with the advance of the Martians, their shields and our failure to combat them, we had to take the risk of experimentation."

"But using it on our own people, for God's sake! How can you justify that!"

"You must believe me, I had nothing to do with that!" The calmness of his voice dismayed me, and I confess I doubted his sincerity.

"So who did? Russell?" I asked. "He gave some sort of order, but even he looked horrified at what happened." I thought back, he had been more upset at the events than Chambers now was. "Someone gave that order, and they should pay for it! And what of his allies? Even if he gave the order, they pulled the trigger, and should share in the guilt."

Chambers nodded. "So let us find out." He led the way out of the room, and we went in search of Russell.

"I promise you," Chambers repeated as we walked, "I did not even realise that the ray was in a working state. Russell will face the consequences of his actions, if he had anything to do with it."

We found Russell on his way to the camp's infirmary. His face was drawn, lips tight and he bore a sadness in his eyes. My anger still boiling, I almost punched him despite his apparent despair.

"Was this your doing?" I shouted, my face mere inches from his own. He shrank back, cowed for the first time since I'd met him. "You worked on the heat-ray in secret, didn't tell anyone that it was working, and the first we learn of it is when it murders our fellow men and women!"

He regained his composure and leaned in to meet me eye to eye. "And what of the tens of thousands already dead at the hands of the Martians, the millions more to come? You don't cry for them. If we can fight back, then I will not hesitate to do what is necessary."

I stared at him agog. "So you admit you ordered this? But this was not fighting back, it was not fighting anyone. It was a massacre of the innocents! And so many of them, I saw them at the gates each time I left my rooms, all they wanted was to be safe... and the poor children!" I fought back tears. Now was not the time for sadness.

"No!" Russell shouted. "I ordered warning shots. A few rounds of machine-gun fire above their heads shifted that crowd. If that warning had not worked, then a few well-aimed rounds at the ringleaders, perhaps, but not this! It looks as if our efforts to root out the Martian sympathisers weren't as effective as we thought. Someone took matters into their own hands. I thank the Lord that only a half-dozen died."

"Only half a dozen? And what do you mean, someone? Who? They must answer for this!"

Russell's face returned to its glum countenance. "They... have already suffered the consequences," he mumbled.

"What? Don't tell me you had them shot!" I said. He shook his head and indicated I should follow him.

The infirmary, or sick-bay as the soldiers referred to it, had barely been used since our arrival. Only a few cuts and scrapes had needed treating, and there were no major injuries requiring use of the facility. Now, however, one of the many beds was occupied, shielded from sight by drawn curtains. Russell led me over and pulled back the drapes. I gasped in horror.

The man in the bed was dying. That much was clear to me instantly, even without medical training. His skin was red and burnt as if he'd spent too long in the sun, blistering on his hands and face. His skin beneath the burns looked pallid, his eyes were closed, and he writhed in pain despite the morphine drip inserted into his arm. I could not tell whether or not he was conscious, but his agony was obviously overwhelming.

"What happened to him?" I asked.

"The power source of the heat-ray," Russell answered. "It operates on the Becquerel principle, the radio-active breakdown of certain elements and is very dangerous to life." He explained that the operation of the heat-ray required such quantities of power that no other source of energy would do. "This was the one who fired it."

"Why?" I asked. "Why would someone countenance an act like this against their brother man?"

Russell handed me a page of scrawled notes. "We found this in his quarters."

I scanned the letter. It proclaimed the man in the bed before me to be a 'soldier for the cause,' willing to do whatever was required to bring about God's plan to cleanse the earth for his chosen ones.

Russell was still talking. "I don't justify what he did, but now we know enough about the heat-ray to use it, and also know more about the cost it entails."

Chambers stood at the end of the man's bed, regarding him with sadness.

Russell spoke more quietly. "We had nowhere to put that many people, no-one to spare to look after children. And we gave them warnings, told them to leave."

"So it's their own damn fault?" I exploded, only to be shushed by a nurse. I continued in a hoarse whisper. "Should they have just gone home and waited for the Martians to take them and drain them dry?"

"If that was to be their fate, this might have been kinder," Chambers suggested.

"Six lives, gone. And for what, a damned air pump?"

"We need all the information we can get," Russell said. "If that box can neutralise the effects of the black smoke, we can protect ourselves and our Ironclads too."

"We have gas masks, they suffice to do that," I said, and my heart sank at the look Russell and Chambers gave one another. "They don't?"

"They may," Chambers conceded. "As best as we can tell, given none of the smoke survived in its original form. The government felt that giving the populace some hope was better than none."

"False hope," I said, and stormed out of the room, unable to look him in the eye.

I needed the joy of true human company again and went back to my quarters. Amy was waiting for me there. As soon as I walked into the room, she dashed across the floor to me. I held out my arms to embrace her, but she dodged my efforts and pummelled me with her balled up fists.

"How could you?" she cried. "You promised me you wouldn't go out, wouldn't take any risks, and yet I awake to find you gone after all. I had to ask Chambers where you were, and he couldn't hide his surprise that I didn't know. Do you know how that made me feel?"

"Did he tell you why?" I asked, grabbing her wrists to stop her attack. "That my brother might be in peril, and that this expedition might have been crucial to turning the tide in our favour?"

Doubt flicked across her face for a moment and I knew he had not. It was a mere moment before her anger returned. "Why did that mean that you had to go?" she countered. "There are professional soldiers here, trained for such duties. Let them do their jobs!" She struggled against my grip, and I released her hands and braced myself for another assault, which did not come.

"And what is my job here?" I asked her. "To write another account, perhaps? And who shall read it, if none survive? It might have been foolish," she scoffed at this, "but in the heat of the moment, I could see no higher calling for me to follow. And it was worthwhile. We have now made a discovery which might prove critical to our defence, and I have contributed something to safeguard my family. I make no apologies for that."

We stared at each other for a long moment, neither of us willing to speak. Eventually, Amy broke the silence.

"I heard what happened at the gate, thank goodness you're alright," she said. "Did they really...?" I nodded, and she cried for a moment before she wiped the tears away and regarded me with her mouth drawn tight. "How many?"

"Six, they tell me. Six innocent lives lost to a lunatic who thinks the Martians are some sort of messenger from God."

"As if there was any of God's love in that man," Amy sniffed. "Or in any of their kind."

"I just hope he was the last of them."

Chapter Fourteen

Flight

After a restless night, the few hours of sleep I managed to snatch disturbed by dreams of screaming, I was in no mood for any more surprises. Over breakfast, I tried to put the thoughts of the previous day's events behind me, and focus on the future. My anger with Chambers and Russell notwithstanding, we still had the problem of the newly arrived Martian to consider. The previous day's events had proven that sending out an Ironclad would have been futile, if we even had one to deploy. The same would be true of a battalion of soldiers, no matter what we could arm them with. Only one weapon at our disposal could threaten the machine, the heat-ray. And even if it were not suicide for whoever operated it, there was no way to turn that device against the Martian unless it drew closer. It had remained a mile or more from the camp since our return; whether it was unaware of the site's importance, thought us unworthy of investigation, or had seen the use of our own heat-ray and feared approaching was unclear, but we couldn't let it remain so close to our base of operations. The idea that the firing of that terrible weapon might have saved us was unbearable, and I tried to put it from my mind.

Reluctantly, I re-joined the planning efforts, aware that the fate of Mankind stood in the balance and such grand stakes required us to all work together no matter what our disagreements. Meeting up with Chambers and Russell I evaded mention of the events the previous day, and they did not bring up the matter either. We kept our discussion to the matter at hand, and while tense, our conversation was at least civil.

I asked what they planned to bring down the fighting machine on our doorstep, enquiring about the availability of another Ironclad, or the feasibility of laying explosives as a trap.

I then learned of another contingency that had been devised, this one remarkably similar to what Chambers and I had discussed in the map room. There were small teams of men, saboteurs or guerrilla fighters who had gone to ground the moment the cylinders landed. They had sheltered in small bunkers, caves or dug-outs and lain low until the tripods reached their territory. At that point, they placed artillery shells along choke-points and connected them to trip-wires. When a tripod came across the wire, it would trigger the explosive. Reports from these fighters were few, owning to their clandestine nature and remoteness from telegraph equipment, but observer stations reported a few tripods downed by 'ground-level explosions' and a few of the mechanical beasts were removed from the planning map. Sadly, too few to make any actual difference.

It would have delighted me to watch similar tactics attempted against our new neighbour, but I was to be surprised yet again by the revelation of a secret.

We had a flying machine.

Before the initial arrival of the Martians, we had made some good progress in the field of gliders, and rumours abounded of intrepid aviators who had strapped small, powerful steam engines to their aircraft. No-one with any scientific understanding truly believed these efforts to achieve powered flight could have succeeded, as they would be hampered because the more powerful an engine was made, the heavier it also was. The ratio between these two measures was the limiting factor in a successful aircraft, and the state of technology was such that it was infeasible to lift the aircraft, engine and aviator from the ground. Should a man wish to add guns to his machine, this increased the weight dramatically, which rendered any air-borne weapon (let alone any thought of armouring the pilot) unimaginable.

With the Martian energy source, so recently employed in the production of our own heat-ray, Russell had solved this problem. In a workshop adjoining the Ironclad sheds, work had been continuing on a suitable vehicle amid the utmost secrecy, and it was this which Russell showed us now.

What rolled out of the building and stood in the afternoon sun was a baffling agglomeration of gleaming metal and painted cloth almost twenty feet long and slightly wider across the tips of its wings. Most of the machine's bulk comprised a pair of these wings, stacked one above the other. Bracing wires spanned the gap between, criss-crossing each other and confusing the eye. It put me in mind of a child's box-kite, grown to massive size.

In front stretched two long metal rails which held smaller wings at their ends, with cables and yet more braces back to the primary structure. At the rear were two shorter rails with skids on the bottom, which left shallow gouges in the earth as men hauled the contraption along. Beneath the wings were wheels upon which it bounced and juddered over the uneven terrain, and two large gun-barrels pointing forwards sat about a third of the way out towards the tips. A propellor sat behind all of this attached by chain to what looked like a small diesel engine at the rear.

An open cabin sat in the centre of the structure between the wings, presumably where the intrepid aviator would sit confined by the braces, wires and cables. The space looked extremely cramped, with one seat facing forwards being designated for the pilot, and one facing rearwards. Directly above their heads, a large metal bulge occupied the mid-point of the topmost wing, and curious tendrils of the same metal snaked across the upper surface with no discernable pattern. It gleamed strangely, glistening as if wet despite the absence of dew.

"Is that the metal they make the tripods from?" I asked.

Russell nodded. "We have a small supply of this unique variant from the last invasion. It has some rather peculiar properties which are required for this machine to operate."

Chambers was staring at the machine in awe, and walked around, examining it from every angle. When he came close to the root of the wings, he stretched up his hand towards the metal. Before I could warn him against it, he pressed his palm against the curious substance.

Nothing happened. "It's warm!" he exclaimed.

"The Martian energy source produces great heat — among other energies. Those are channelled through the web you see and produce a gravity insulating effect."

"Is this the same source that the heat-ray used? Are we safe?" I asked.

"It's quiescent now," Russell replied. "When it's not in use, we can move it around and handle it. But when we power it up, that's when it becomes a danger. We have sufficient protection for the pilot and the engine operator — you see the lead plate above their heads? — but any more would render it too heavy to fly. So when this launches, we must all be at a safe distance."

"Did you say gravity insulation?" Chambers asked, peering at the filigree atop the wings. "How does that work?"

"Very well," Russell replied, "just don't ask anyone to explain it. Our physicist had a breakdown just trying, so our engineers try not to think about it too much."

"So it just ignores gravity and floats about like a balloon? Why do you need the wings?" I asked.

"The motor drives the craft forwards, and it flies in the usual manner. The Martian stuff just removes its weight, or reduces it, I should say, to let us get it off the ground. Plus, if something goes wrong, it can still glide to the ground."

"So you'll fly over the Martian and use the heat-ray on him at close range?" I asked.

Russell shook his head. "The reactor, flight and the projector apparatus together would be too heavy, and require more power than this can provide. We're at the absolute limits of what we can achieve as it is. We hope that the Martian shield will only protect them against attacks from below, or at least will be easier to breach from above. Hence the two guns. Ideally, we'd drive him closer with the aircraft and then use the heat-ray from the gates, but with only one source…"

"We had reports of Ironclads failing to break the shield when firing from high ground," I reminded him. "You're taking a hell of a risk assuming that this contraption can do any better."

"It's a long-shot," Chambers agreed. "But we can hardly let him wander the land."

———◄O►———

"Any other secrets you've been keeping from us?" Chambers asked Russell as men dragged the flying machine into position. I had been wondering the same myself. Two revelations in as many days were disconcerting.

"If I told you, they wouldn't be secrets," Russell replied enigmatically. I would have pressed him for clarity, but my mind was on the aircraft and the pilot and operator as they walked alongside. They wore thick woollen clothing, silk gloves and leather goggles to protect against the chill of the wind as they flew, and were so focused on the task ahead of themselves that I dared not to interrupt their thoughts to introduce myself.

We reached the gates of the camp; they swung open, and men bearing weapons surged forth to take up positions covering the entrance. All eyes were on the Martian, trusting that its fear of our heat-ray would keep it far enough away to allow us to prepare in safety. Once the machine-guns and mortars were in position, a handful of mechanics pushed the aircraft out into the road to a distance of a few hundred feet from the gate, this being deemed a safe enough distance. They then dashed forward, clearing debris and rubble from the road to give the pilot a smooth, clear run for take-off. Not one man of them hesitated as they drew ever closer to the Martian fighting machine, and my heart was in my mouth as I watched them working, all the time keeping one eye on the adversary for any sign of interest in our proceedings. Before long, they had checked and cleared a sufficient stretch of road and they scurried back inside the gates, which closed behind them.

"Will those gunners be safe? They are much closer than us," I asked, thoughts of the hospitalised man still crowding my mind.

"They should be," Russell replied, "the effects are at their worst directly behind the craft, and at relatively short range. They're at more risk from the damn thing dropping on their heads."

Through binoculars from the top of the observation tower, I watched the pilot and the man who would operate the Martian power source clamber carefully into the cabin. This operator was the scientist who had uncovered the secrets of this device's operation, and one of only a handful of men capable of controlling it. Negotiating the maze of wires and strengthening cables looked more like an assault course, and I realised these men could never escape the craft quickly in any kind of emergency.

The Martian now had stopped pacing and was (as far as one could judge its motives at all) monitoring the proceedings with care. Every man in camp was on tenterhooks, holding his breath, waiting for its sudden movement towards us, or the stab of the heat-ray at the aircraft. Nothing came. Perhaps these creatures were as curious as we were, maybe it was keen to see what novelty we primitive inhabitants of this planet might have developed.

The noisy clatter of the diesel engine broke the silence, and I must confess I jumped at the sudden sound. After a moment, the propeller on the rear of the craft spun, driven by the chain from the motor. Then a shimmering haze appeared, as on a hot summer's day, blurring my view of the machine as the heat of the Martian energy source built. A low whine accompanied this development, rising in pitch and volume as the power grew. Each moment, the noise grew, piercing our ears with intolerable volume. The pilot and engineer had been wearing ear defenders, but the sound must surely still have deafened them. I clasped my hands over my ears, dropping the binoculars to hang on their string around my neck. I thought I saw a distortion beneath the wings, as if viewing the scene beyond through a lens or a distorting mirror.

Imperceptibly at first, the machine wobbled and swayed, as if yearning to leave the ground behind it. The propeller span up to full speed, and the entire craft rolled forward, gathering speed with each yard covered. Trundling over the once melted surface of the road offered little resistance and soon the machine was as fast as a galloping horse — then it seemed to strain for the sky, its nose lifting and sparks rising from the skids in the rear as they dragged along the ground. The craft began making little hops upward repeatedly until with a lumbering wobble it lifted from the ground, leaving behind the wheels to slew from the road and crash into a ditch. By now the tower was vibrating in sympathy with the sound of the engine, and I was glad when that diminished as the flying machine moved further away and slowly arced towards the Martian.

Chapter Fifteen

Airborne

E ven now it was airborne, the craft moved so slowly I was sure it would simply drop from the sky, each lurch and dip of the long wings accompanied by a skip of my heart with fear that this was the moment it would crash. But gradually, inch by painful inch, it gained height — and drew towards its enemy. When it had launched, the Martian had been facing it. As it drew closer, the fighting machine turned to keep it in view, and to all appearances, regarded it curiously. We all held our breath as the aircraft closed the distance; we knew the range of the machine guns would not match that of the Martian's heat-ray, and prayed that curiosity would stay its fire until we could bring our own weapons to bear. The pilot approached the Martian while constantly weaving from side to side in the hopes it would prevent the tripod from hitting him. The pilot could steer the guns beneath the wing within a small arc, and they never wavered from their target. By now the craft was about ten feet higher than the top of the Martian, and you could have heard a pin drop in the camp as we all hoped and prayed that the shields wouldn't extend over the top of the carapace.

Puffs of smoke from the gun barrels — the sound delayed by the distance — let us know he had fired the first shots. Sparks flew from the top of the Martian — they'd hit! But a ricochet wouldn't do any good, we needed more. The pilot kept the guns trained on the target as long as possible, but as he drew close to the Martian, he was forced to break off.

Slowly, so slowly, the pilot increased the distance between himself and the tripod before swinging around for another run. The entire time, the Martian kept turning to face him, seemingly unconcerned. Why would he not fire? Did he know we posed no threat?

The guns barked again, this time the pilot's aim had improved —
no doubt he was getting the hang of his curious machine. Sparks
flew from the tripod's head again in a trail towards what passed for
its eyes, the large glassy window-like shapes on the front. When
one cracked and then shattered, a cheer went up from the camp
— one which grew louder when a curious gas emanated from the
opening. We could hurt them!

One more pass, and this time the Martian swiped at the flying
machine with one of its long tentacles — the thick metal rope
snapping through the air so fast as to blur with motion, but
somehow the pilot judged the claw's approach and dodged it. This
threw off his aim, however, and we saw the dirt behind the Martian
spray up into the air as the bullets passed harmlessly by.

The brave pilot came around for yet another pass, dodging this
way and that as he approached, wary of another tentacle coming at
him. A door on the lower portion of the Martian's carapace opened
up, and a tentacle probed inside it before emerging with a heat-ray
projector in its grasp. We all fell silent and watched in fear.

The pilot saw the threat and withdrew, still weaving about in
the sky like a drunk, first this way then that, avoiding any pattern
that the Martian might use to predict his next location. He circled
the Martian slowly at a safe distance, was he trying to goad it into
attacking? No! He banked hard, forcing his craft around so that the
guns managed a shot at the tripod from range once more before
banking back away and opening up the distance. The first time he
tried this manoeuvre he missed, but the second time his aim was
true.

Sparks once again flew from the carapace, only a few before
the rounds found their target in the gaping hole which resembled
nothing so much as a vast, lidless eye.

The machine stumbled, its legs giving way beneath it, and
toppled heavily into the woods beside the road. The jubilation in
the camp was unrestrained, an observer would have thought we
had won the entire war right there and then.

Our hero made a wobbling circuit of the fallen machine, looking
for signs of life or movement, even as Russell assembled a team of
men to go out to investigate the tripod. No sooner was the order
given, however, than the aircraft jolted, as if hit. It rolled to port,
coming to an angle of thirty degrees before the pilot wrenched it
back under control, first overcompensating and rolling starboard
before pulling it level once more.

Then the wings caught fire.

Within seconds the canvas was burned through, the plane
plummeting towards the earth trailing smoke and flame. It hit

the ground hard, the metal frame folding like wet straw and the cabin crumpling under the force of the impact. Even without my binoculars, I knew there was no hope for the men inside.

A second Martian fighting machine hove into view — heat-ray projector held aloft, trained on the wreckage. A cry of 'ulla' echoed over the plain as it stood over the ruins of our best hope for salvation.

Such despair would have been unbearable as it was, but coming on the heels of such a victory made it intolerable. We had proven the tripods vulnerable to assault from above, verified that with the right approach and the best of our ingenuity we might master the skies, only to have all hope dashed away in an instant.

The ambushing Martian took position above the wreckage of its comrade and our flying machine. We could not investigate either one, nor retrieve our dead with an enemy so close to our own gates. We had traded our flying machine and the energy source it contained for one of their tripods. Even if we had a limitless supply of either, it would have been a poor trade — that we had lost the only example of each was devastating.

After the initial shock of our defeat wore off, the guns and mortars deployed to protect the aircraft's rollout opened fire at the new arrival, to limited effect. The creature would be out of range of all but the largest artillery.

"Damn it, cease fire!" Russell shouted. If the men heard him, they gave no sign of it, but continued their fruitless activity. Chambers collared a Sergeant-Major and sent him out to regain control, and we watched him lashing about himself with his pace stick, restoring order to the ranks. Glumly the soldiers dragged their equipment back into the camp and slammed the gates shut, for what little protection they might afford.

Recriminations started immediately — everyone blaming some other fellow for the disaster to deflect their own feelings of despondency and failure. Russell was quick to cast blame in all directions, doubtless sensing as we all did that most of the responsibility for our loss could be justifiably laid at his own feet. He regaled anyone who would listen, or indeed stand still for long enough in his vicinity, with endless reasons why the disaster was not his fault. To listen to him, it was alternately a result of the pilot's errors, the poor design of the aircraft, underpowered guns, the government exiled in Wiltshire, anyone but himself of course.

Chambers had no time for blame-throwing or name-calling and took himself out of the discussion as soon as the gates were closed. I later found him sat quietly with the wives of the lost men, attempting to console them and reassure them that their husband's sacrifices would not be in vain. Russell took the opportunity to shift the blame onto Chambers' shoulders, seizing on the latter's compassion as an admission of guilt in some manner. It is to Chambers' credit that he did not rise to the bait, and refrained from responding. However, among most of the camp who had witnessed the events, such arguments found traction, and it forced me to step to his defence when the most egregious of rumours reached me.

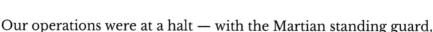

Our operations were at a halt — with the Martian standing guard, we had no opportunity to leave the camp, and no-one could come to our aid even if there was anyone to do so.

In order to avoid the stares and whispered sneers of the camp's staff, Chambers spent the rest of the day and much of the night sequestered in the communications room trying to re-establish communications with the government in Wiltshire. His efforts were in vain, and even attempts to reach some of the more local stations failed. We feared the Martians must have discovered and cut our telegraph lines. Radio worked intermittently, but the range appeared very limited. He and I believed the Martians were preventing our signals from travelling, though we were at a loss to explain how. Loud whistling sounds travelling up and down the scale emanated from our wireless equipment on certain frequencies, passing into inaudibility at the extremes. We presumed that these were a communication between the Martian machines, or the machines and their bases of operations, but could not determine a pattern within the whistles. They might simply have been designed to prevent our own use of the radio.

That morning was one of the coldest so far that autumn, fairly matching the mood in the camp. Tempers already frayed by the events of the previous day were now at breaking point — a night without sleep and a chill mist covering the area around the camp tested even the strongest wills.

Chambers had some limited success on the short-wave after dawn. Whether because of the Martian jamming attempts faltering or some atmospheric quirk, I cannot say, but he heard a few brief reports from the Continent. Sadly, there was little enough among these messages to lift our spirits.

It appeared that the Martians had repeated the coordinated attack we had seen in our country across the whole of Europe, and at almost exactly the same time. In other circumstances, the ability of an invading army to synchronise their movements so precisely over such a large area might have impressed me, but at this moment it merely shone a brighter light upon our own failings.

A radio operator just outside Paris reported the city had fallen on the first day to a force of four fighting machines, deploying the dreadful black smoke on the outskirts and allowing the prevailing winds to carry it through the ancient streets. He had little information from the rest of the country, but this was sufficient evidence for him that the whole of France had fallen.

A similar story had played out across the Low Countries, Italy and a few of the more easterly nations. The tripods had made few inroads into the Alps, whether because of the unsuitability of their locomotive manner for the terrain or a dislike of the cold temperatures at altitude, was unknown. Very few people had found sanctuary there before the attacks had begun.

We could not contact Spain or Germany, but some third-hand reports suggested that forces had halted the Martians briefly outside Berlin, the defences there being successful in bringing down two or three of the machines. The lack of communication now suggested that such a victory had been short-lived.

The message was obvious. Europe had fallen, and even the hardiest optimist would be unlikely to claim that the wider world was untouched.

Chapter Sixteen

Desperation

Chambers and Russell were barely on speaking terms after the disaster the previous day, and I appointed myself to act as an intermediary. Accusations and blame were never far beneath the surface and I found it hard to keep the flow of ideas coming without each immediately being shot down by the other man.

"Can we at least agree," I said, "what the priorities are? Firstly: we ought to reestablish communications with the local area and ideally the government too. Knowledge is power, and we can ask for advice and help if we can speak with our allies. Secondly: reactivate our heat-ray before the alien force realises that we are defenceless and presses their advantage. And thirdly: scout out the local area to determine the Martian's activities and whether our strike on their cylinder had any effect."

"Our only priority," Russell countered, "is to destroy that fighting machine before it wipes us out."

"If we could even do that, it would just invite another retaliation," Chambers piped up. "We should flee and regroup elsewhere."

"And abandon everything here?" Russell replied. "That's cowardice! I would never tolerate desertion in the face of the enemy."

"We're not talking about desertion," Chambers replied. For once, he was standing his ground rather than relying on me to press his point. "It's a strategic retreat from an unwinnable situation."

Russell scoffed, and I realised that they would reach no accord in this manner. Each man had his own ideas and would brook no disagreement from the other, and my efforts to negotiate a middle-ground had so far attracted only scorn.

Eventually I accepted my fate and declared I would play the role of moderator; each man would put forward his suggestions and work to convince me of the rightness of his ideas. Even deciding who would begin was fractious, so I elected to toss a coin. It came down 'heads', and Chambers took the floor.

"We have no Ironclads," he began. "No reactor, and no operator able to run one if we even did. So we have no heat-ray. The nearest artillery is out of range and out of contact. We have no aircraft, and no pilot for one."

"Enough of what we don't have," Russell interrupted. "It does us no good to list our failures. My men are finishing another Ironclad as we speak, and I can operate the reactor." I reminded him to wait his turn, and he reluctantly did.

"We should leave," Chambers said. "Depart for a safer location, somewhere we can regroup with other forces and pool our remaining resources."

"Where?" Russell sneered. "You don't know who else is still alive, let alone able to help us. No, we strike now. Take down the fighting machine and recover our property."

"How do you propose we do that?" I asked. "We could barely take down the first with an Ironclad, or the second with the aircraft." Chambers nodded agreement.

"Hand-to-hand, of course," Russell said, and Chambers laughed. Russell ignored him and pressed on. "We know a few teams brought down tripods with explosives, we do the same. Or string metal chains between the trees to trip them! We wait for cover of night and..."

"Even assuming it stays put until then, what next?" Chambers interrupted. "Walk up and hope they cannot see in the dark?"

"There is cover along the sides of the road. A small team with a shaped charge affix it to the machine's leg and are out of danger in moments."

"You cannot be countenancing this?" Chambers turned to me incredulously. "It'd be suicide! Right now that thing is keeping its distance, but if it feels threatened by us, it will wipe this camp clean in an instant!"

"It still thinks we possess a heat-ray of our own," Russell replied. "The fear of that keeps it at bay."

"But we don't. And if it sees us try to strike, it'll know we're desperate," Chambers said. "We should retreat."

They continued arguing, throwing the same ideas back and forth while I weighed up the alternatives. My mind was churning with the possibilities. What would be the best course of action? Evacuate to an uncertain fate, in the hopes other camps still existed or had fared better than us? Or strike back, risking retaliation once again, hoping to buy time for the rebuilding of our defences? Something nagged at me, some half-noticed or half-remembered detail that might have been important.

Russell was scarlet in the face. "I am the only soldier in this room, and the most senior officer on this base! I decide what the army does, and whatever you do will require our assistance. I can tell you it will not be coming, unless you choose to attack."

"Russell, where did the air pump go?" I asked quietly.

Chambers and I stared at him for a moment, while his mouth opened and closed twice.

"That's classified," he eventually replied.

"I think the time for secrets has passed," I said. "Clearly it's somewhere safe, or you'd never have entrusted that device to it. And the truck that left with it was back within the hour, so it's not too far. Are you still in contact with them?"

It took a while for him to meet my eye. He nodded once.

"How?" Chambers asked in disbelief. "The Martians jam our radio, and we lost telegraphy two days ago."

"Runners," Russell replied. "For vital communications we use messengers."

Chambers looked ready to launch himself over the table at Russell, the meek and almost subservient man I knew was nowhere to be seen.

"How could you?" he cried. "Those men could have been carrying messages all over for us, could have helped us in so many ways! And you kept it all a secret!"

"Now is not the time," I interrupted. "Can this place take our evacuees?" This could be a means to keep Amy safe.

Russell nodded again. He spoke softly, where I expected defiance. "They can take most of us. The expected staff didn't all make it there from London, so there is some capacity."

"Then I have an answer," I said. "Evacuate the women, children and non-essential men while we ask for volunteers to try Russell's attack. We use the assault as a distraction until we're sure non-combatants are all at a safe distance. That way, we'll not be risking anyone who isn't fully aware of the dangers and has chosen to meet them. If we can defeat the Martian, we reclaim our aircraft and power source. If not, we join the evacuation."

They both greeted my proposal with disdain, which gave me confidence it was indeed the best compromise. If one man had approved and not the other, I would have known I had erred.

"So you choose to anger the Martian, while our women and children are out in the open, undefended?" Chambers asked incredulously.

"You're the one who wanted to send them out," Russell replied. "This way we keep the Martian occupied, at least."

I interjected. "They will be guarded as well. So you approve?"

"Not at all," Russell rounded on me. "How many of my soldiers are escorting the cowards? How many will I have left to attack? This will fail without enough men."

"You will have as many as volunteer for your assault," I replied. "The rest will be escorts and guards. Everyone has their part to play if this is to succeed. Speaking of which, I must do my bit. Get to work."

I suspect Russell was considering whether he could order me shot for insubordination if I wasn't a member of the army. I ignored the bluster from my comrades and went in search of my wife.

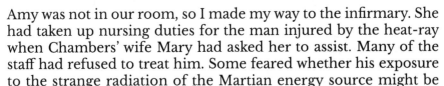

Amy was not in our room, so I made my way to the infirmary. She had taken up nursing duties for the man injured by the heat-ray when Chambers' wife Mary had asked her to assist. Many of the staff had refused to treat him. Some feared whether his exposure to the strange radiation of the Martian energy source might be contagious, while others objected to aiding a confessed traitor to humanity.

Being as kind and caring as I knew her to be, Amy had, of course, agreed immediately. Be he ally or enemy, he was still a human being and she could never pass by when someone was in need. When I arrived, however, I did not see her anywhere.

"Hello?" I called out.

"Just a moment," came her voice from behind the curtain drawn around the bed. The curtain drew back, and I caught a momentary glimpse of the rake-thin fellow in the bed. His skin was grey, his hair fallen out except for a few wisps, and his eyes sunken. He regarded me with a mixture of terror and exhaustion before Amy pulled the curtain closed once more.

"How is he?" I whispered.

She glanced back over her shoulder before leading me further away. She leaned close to whisper to me, her breath warm against my cheek even as her words were cold. "He won't last the week."

The usual sparkle in her eyes that I loved was missing, but she held her head high. I knew she felt better having something useful to contribute, but I wished she had found something less draining and unpleasant on which to spend her attention.

Mindful of not disturbing the invalid, she led me to a small ante-room away from the main ward. A couple of nurses sat there drinking tea. "And how are you?" she asked. "What news from the front?" Her words were light, but her tone was strained.

I explained the plan we had formulated, and thankfully she agreed with my compromise. Where I lost her support was when I explained she would join the exodus.

"You expect me to leave this poor man here, desert him to save myself?"

"You said he is at death's door," I pointed out. "There will be nothing for you to do soon enough."

"I shall not leave," she protested. "Go without me."

"I'm not going anywhere," I explained. "Russell and Chambers will be at each other's throats within an hour if I don't stay, so my duty is clear," I proclaimed.

She scoffed. "Then let them," she said. "What business is it of ours if they can't get along? If in the face of these monsters," she gestured towards the gate and the Martians beyond, "men cannot put aside differences and work to the greater good, then what hope is there for Man?"

"What hope is there if we do not fight?" I countered. "If we all run and hide, we're no better than cowards."

"And yet this is what you tell me to do," she replied. "You think me a coward too?"

"This battle is no place for a woman," I barely noticed the nurses turning to look at us as my voice grew louder. "I will see you in safety!"

"It's no place for a writer, either," she snarled. "How quickly you forget the effect these matters had on you previously. I cannot face nursing you back to sanity again." Now I saw the curious faces turned towards us and motioned her to silence, to no avail. "If you are to send me away, I will have my say first," she continued.

"Say your piece then, and go."

"You fancy yourself a hero, a warrior who rebuffed the first invasion single-handed. Your tales of the privations and troubles you encountered have blinded you to the truth of your experience — you killed only one being, and that a fellow man. I do not say this to be cruel," she added, "but to remind you of the pain and suffering that followed that necessary act." She drew closer and placed her hand on my face. "That moment broke you, shattered your mind and sent you reeling out into the battle to seek not vengeance, not justice, but punishment. You believed you should suffer for your sins, that trauma left you a mere shell — if the bacteria of this world had not left the tripods as empty as you, we would neither one of us be here today."

"What is your point?" I whispered, untrusting of my voice not to break.

"You are not ready for this battle," she replied quietly. Our faces were now so close we could kiss. "And you know better than most men what sacrifices must be made in such fights. You were forced to kill to save yourself once, and it almost took you from me. Do not delude yourself that you can do it again without repercussions."

"It will be a small price to pay, if it keeps you safe," I replied. "And free Man once and for all from this nightmare."

"Then I've lost you," she said sadly. "If any part of you remains after you 'do your duty', then come back to me, but I do not believe you will be my husband again."

<hr />

Conscious of every eye in the place upon my back, I strode from the room without looking over my shoulder. More painful than my wife's goodbye, worse than the tears that sprang to her eyes (and mine, though I dared not let her see) were the thoughts that she might be right. That to play my part in the battle to come would change me for the worst, leave me unable to resume my place at her side. I counselled myself that it was a necessary evil, that just as I had done the unthinkable once before in the service of survival, I would have to do it again.

And I will not countenance an atrocity like that heat-ray, used on our own people, I told myself. *If I am there with Russell, I can hold him back from his worst impulses; Chambers and I together as the voice of reason can restrain him.*

I would soon discover whether I had this strength and ability at all.

Chapter Seventeen

Exodus

I returned to my room, attempting to rest so I might be prepared for nightfall and the planned attack. Sleep eluded me. Arguments flooded my mind, thoughts of words I should have spoken to convince Amy of the necessity of my remaining here, of the need for to her to leave. None of them convinced me, and I lay there wracked with self-doubt until the light faded.

On my way to the canteen, I had watched in the moonlight as an untidy group of figures gathered towards the rear of the camp, away from the Martian. I issued a silent prayer that they would be safe. Whether or not Amy was among them, I could not tell in the gloom.

Russell, Chambers and a few volunteers were already gathered when I arrived. "Now we're all here," Russell said pointedly, "I can begin." A make-shift blackboard had been painted on one wall of the room a few days earlier and he approached it now. Clearly, despite his words, they had already begun planning without me. The crude outline of our camp sat at the centre, and symbols marked the locations of the flyer, downed Martian and the remaining war machine. Russell pulled a pointer from his pocket, extended it, and tapped it against the wall. "First platoon will be here," a tap, "with mortars and flash bangs to draw the Martian away. He will approach them, directly into the line of claymores here," another tap, "laid by second platoon who will hide in this ditch," tap. "When he crosses the killing line, they will detonate the claymores, tripping and causing him to fall. Then third platoon emerge from their concealment here," tap, "and affix the shaped charges." Here he gestured behind us with his pointer, and I turned to see satchels arranged on the tables. "The legs aren't shielded, so there won't be any difficulty. Those charges are on a ten-second fuse — as soon as they're attached, it starts running. If I was you, I'd do the same." He chuckled at his own joke, but no-one joined him.

"You aren't going with chains to trip it?" I asked.

"We don't have any strong enough, and they'd be noisy," Russell explained.

"And what if it doesn't fall for the trap?" Chambers asked. "A few mortars can't hurt it, and it seems likely it knows that. Why would it bother to pursue first platoon?" A few of the volunteers shifted uncomfortably at the idea, and I considered admitting I had wondered the same.

"Their only goal is to wipe us out," Russell retorted. "If it sees a few troublemakers, it won't hesitate. Like stamping on an anthill." The youngest volunteer was turning white.

"Is everyone clear on what they are to do?" I asked, before thoughts of flight entered their minds. A chorus of assent rose from most of the assembled men, with tight-lipped nods from the rest. "Grab your gear and let's get moving."

The sound of the first flash-bang was the signal for the evacuees to leave the camp. They streamed out of the rear, out of sight of us in the darkness and hopefully invisible to the Martian too, as the movements and commotion raised by our diversionary force drew its attention. Chambers, Russell and I watched anxiously from the camp watchtower as the sergeants and their men put the plan into action. Mortar fire, flashes of light and loud bangs appeared to be proving Russell correct — the Martian could not resist the opportunity it saw to punish a small group of us, and spun on its three legs to ready a pursuit as they scattered as planned. Metal flashed in the moonlight as it spun and attacked.

Tentacles struck out from the carapace, grabbing at one man before he could react. The Martian lifted him high into the air, and we heard his screams even over the intervening distance. The rest of the men could do nothing to help him as the tentacle dashed him against a tree, silencing his scream for good. It dropped the body with a sickening thud and set off in pursuit of the next man.

Two paces into its stride, and before it could gather much speed, the claymores fired with a low thumping noise we all felt in our chests. One cluster missed entirely, but the other was close enough to one leg to cause a minor buckling — the centre of weight of the Martian rocking away from its accustomed position over the middle of the three limbs and forcing it to stumble. With a shout, the third platoon dashed from their concealment and strapped their charges to the damaged leg.

As they retreated, the heat-ray fired at them. They'd scattered, hoping to confuse the creature long enough to escape, but it spun the projector over every one of them, the flames springing up so fast as to blind us, which mercifully spared us the sight of the men's demise. It then waved the fiery beam around wildly, as a man bats about himself when he stumbles into a hornet's nest, flailing against the irritants that beset him. Shouts and screams were quickly silenced as the flames took hold, and the fleeing figures became fewer and fewer.

Then the charges fired; the damaged leg folded like paper, and the machine tumbled to the ground. What remained of the volunteers circled it warily until convinced that the heat-ray had been stilled.

Rifles at the ready, they surrounded the downed machine, prepared to fire if something should emerge. They closed the distance carefully, alert for any movement, but none came. A figure drew an axe from his pack and smashed at the windows of the machine, the ringing blows carrying on the wind. It bounced off, but a volley of fire from the men's rifles cracked the glass. A few more blows of the axe opened a hole, and someone threw a grenade inside the carapace, the men retreating to a safe distance.

"No, damn it!" Russell shouted, but there was no sign of anyone having heard him. It was too late, as the grenade exploded with a muffled crump and smoke and flame billowed from the downed machine. "Idiots! How are we to learn anything if they blow the damn thing up?"

"You'd rather they left that thing inside alive?" Chambers said. "We've lost enough men already to this assault, don't you think?"

Given the success of the operation, Chambers ordered a flare fired into the air above the camp, which was the signal to the evacuees that they might return safely. Most elected to do so, but a few pressed on in search of the different and hopefully better refuge. Those who came back later reported that those few had feared further recriminations from the invaders.

Russell was still furious at the destruction of the Martian, but consoled himself that at least it had not exploded the power source.

"If that had blown up, who knows what would have happened," he said.

With little enough left to explore inside the fighting machine, Russell and his team focused their attention on our crashed flyer. Chambers insisted that they not start their investigation until we had removed the remains of the pilot and reactor operator with dignity. Russell protested at first, but demurred when his own men refused to proceed with his orders, standing with their caps in hands as a make-shift funeral guard.

Once work began, Russell quickly established that the reactor was still functional, if damaged. The dangers within were still contained, but there would be work to do in order to bring it back into operation. The flying machine itself, however, was another matter. As feared, the impact with the ground had bent or broken practically every spar on the fuselage; the wings had sheared off and snapped, and the fabric covering was burned away. Only the curious Martian metal that covered the reactor and the wings had survived the intense heat that had brought the aircraft down.

We needed heavy lifting equipment to extract the reactor from the wreckage, and Russell pressed the returned evacuees into service to bring it out of the camp. Others used crowbars and long wooden sticks to lever the wreckage up to allow chains and lifting straps to be connected. All the while, we kept a nervous watch on the horizon, no-one truly believing that the Martian had not issued a distress call before its defeat.

By mid-afternoon the reactor was back in the engineer's sheds, and Russell was exploring the downed Martians, hoping something had survived intact. His glowering and irritable demeanour when he returned told us all that nothing had.

<hr />

I left Russell and Chambers to take stock of our supplies, while I went to attempt smoothing matters over with Amy. She was not in our room, or the canteen, so once more I made my way to the infirmary.

Chambers' wife Mary was there, tending to a handful of injured men from the earlier attack. Most of their wounds were minor, superficial burns and a few shrapnel injuries. Of Amy, there was no sign.

"She remained with the evacuees," Mary informed me, with surprise. "They pressed on, even after the recall. Corporal Jones, that sympathiser, was being transported hoping to find better care at their destination. I think she believed that her purpose might be better served with him, and them, than here. She told me you had agreed it was for the best."

I had indeed told her to go, but I had assumed she would return when it was safe. I had not seriously believed that she would choose to leave me, especially under such circumstances.

"Jones was deteriorating," Mary continued. "She felt bound to care for him if she could. I offered to assist her, of course, but she insisted I return. She said that this camp would have a greater need for a trained nurse than one pressed into service so lately."

Mary's words soothed me a little, I might allow myself to believe that Amy had chosen the altruistic path, decided to care for one in dire need, rather than abandoning me. But I knew the truth, that I had driven her from me.

I had barely considered my next actions when a messenger arrived to fetch me.

I found Russell and Chambers at each other's throats once again, and it took some time before I fully understood their argument. Russell, it seems, was all for evacuating the recovered reactor to the other location our evacuees had headed for. Still, he refused to give us much information about it but merely hinted that the people there would make better use of it than we could. His infuriating innuendo that this other station was more effective than our own had rankled with Chambers, naturally, who insisted that we restore the heat-ray here to operation as a matter of urgency.

My immediate thought was that this gave me an excuse to pursue Amy. If I sided with Russell, I could offer to accompany him and his prize to their base and reunite with my wife. But as tempting as that opportunity might be, I had to put selfishness aside and consider what was the best approach to the situation at hand for all men, and not merely myself.

"I am minded to agree with Chambers," I said eventually, to Russell's inevitable annoyance. "Removing our last defence here would be suicidal for those left behind, and besides you already dismissed evacuating everyone as unacceptable. But once again, can we not find a compromise? We know we can mount the reactor to an airframe, but why should we not attach it to an Ironclad?" With knowledge of the reactor's operations limited only to Russell, I needed to keep him on our side. Tempting him with new challenges might prove the best way to do so.

Russell laughed. "They will not go any faster no matter how you power them."

"I said compromise, and I meant it. Why not mount a heat-ray on a mobile platform? We know they can fire out through their shields, so doubtless we can fire in."

Both men stared at me for a moment before breaking out in grins. Why they had not thought of this themselves I couldn't say, but I wished I had as easy a solution to the problems in my marriage as I did for the relationship between these two men.

Chapter Eighteen

Retribution

That first day after downing the fighting machine was terrifying. Every man present must have worked at only half-speed, frequently interrupting his activities to scan the horizon. I caught myself gazing over the walls of our camp for longer than I realised, instead of working. I scarcely believed that the Martians could be unaware of the loss of another machine and concluded that they did now view our little camp as a threat. No doubt they were deciding how best to deal with us, but their reluctance to engage us was a blessing. Every day we had to work on the preparations of the new Ironclad was vital.

After that first day passed with no interference, Chambers had insisted a group of volunteers lay mines and claymores along the obvious approaches to the camp, as a protection against the future attack we all knew had to be inevitable. They came back reporting the first sightings of the Red Weed we were familiar with from our previous encounter with the invaders. Russell ordered the volunteers back out, and samples brought to him. Grumbling, they did as he asked and returned with a few bucketfuls of the tenacious stuff. I had not been able to scrutinise it the last time, and took the opportunity now.

In colour, it reminded me of nothing so much as drying blood, a deep crimson with brown tones. In shape, it resembled some of the more exotic succulents I have seen at Kew, with small bulbous and waxy tendrils in place of leaves. When pinched or cut, these oozed a thick reddish liquid disturbingly akin to blood, and which emitted a distinct metallic scent. The trunks or branches of the growth were similarly waxen, something Chambers suggested was an adaptation to the small quantities of water to be found on Mars.

"Rounded, almost tubular leaves minimise the surface area, and reduce the amount of moisture lost," he explained, "and the thick skin reduces it still further. And look, the roots are similarly coated unto the tips, which are more like the roots we know from our own plants. That must be where it collects water. If that thing gets the upper hand, we'll not be able to grow our own crops," he pointed out, "so it's vital we stop it before it takes hold."

"Might the same blight as last time not doom it again?" I asked.

"I would imagine not," Chambers replied. "Most likely they have adapted it to suit the known conditions, as they have their equipment and presumably themselves."

"The Martians do not appear to use it as a source of food or for any other purpose, so they may not have intended it to accompany them at all. If it is a stowaway..."

"We shall soon know," Chambers said. "But I fear the worst, and we must prepare accordingly."

We knew from the previous infestation that when the weed discovered a source of water, its growth was so quick as to be almost observable by the unaided eye. I procured a small sample from Russell for my experimentation while he transferred the rest to his remote lab with a small crew of scientists under orders to find a means to prevent it from taking root.

I convinced one of these scientists to take with him a note for Amy, in which I apologised for my behaviour and implored her to return to me. Naturally, considering the situation I urged her not to do so alone, but since the communication between Russell and his scientists was through couriers rather than radio I assumed she could find her way back here with one of them as escort if she so desired.

The kind fellow who took my note promised to allow his couriers to act as relays for any future messages, and to keep the matter between ourselves. Russell would not have approved of my subversion of his lines of communication, for any purpose.

※

There was an occasional sighting of a Martian fighting machine on the horizon during the next few days, though none approached us directly. Each time one loomed into view, all work halted at the sound of the warning whistles, every eye turned on the machine until it dipped out of sight.

The only men who did not interrupt their activities were those working around the clock on the modifications to the almost completed Ironclad. I had asked if I might observe the construction work, ostensibly to document it but also partially for my curiosity. Russell refused, convinced I would get in the way and slow down the work. He would brook no interruptions to the activity, and had pressed his crews to work ever longer shifts to complete it. There were few protests, everyone being acutely aware of the dangers we faced and that these men were the primary hope for us all, but such long days engaged in such arduous work inevitably led to accidents. The infirmary was soon pressed back into action again, mostly for minor injuries such as cuts and scrapes or crushed fingers. However, one cold morning a lifting cable slipped loose from its mounting, and the entire upper turret swung loose. Tens of tons of hardened steel whipped across the workshop, flinging men aside before slamming into the wall and crushing two unfortunates between its bulk and the cinder blocks that finally arrested its movement. I was glad that I had not argued more forcefully with Russell and insisted on observing.

Chamber's wife Mary and the two doctors were rushed off their feet in the aftermath, tending to those they could help and making the rest comfortable.

"I wish Amy were still here," Mary said in an unguarded moment, before catching herself. "I'm sorry, I just meant..." she continued.

"I understand," I replied. "I miss her dreadfully, but I know that if she were here she would help you at all hours. If I get the opportunity, I will pass on your good wishes."

Where previously Russell had pushed ahead at full speed, he was now forced to slow the pace of work because of the accident. I would like to believe that he felt unable to stomach the risk to his workers, but I suspect he had calculated the impact on his schedule of another mishap and made an emotionless decision to minimise delays. Whenever I dropped in to speak to him, I found him frosty but accommodating to my questions, so long as he didn't find them foolish or trivial. From him I learned that they had added enough of the strange Martian metal to the iron shell of the machine to offer adequate protection against the dangers of the reactor to the men inside. I could not draw him on the precise definition of 'adequate', but I figured he meant the greater dangers to the crew would come from the Martians. If they survived long enough to risk suffering ill-effects from the reactor, then they would probably consider themselves fortunate.

Before too long, the Ironclad was ready for testing, and the men christened it the *Joseph Cooper* after the first of their comrades to fall assaulting the Martians. Russell thought it sentimental to name them at all, but for once didn't speak this belief out loud.

Lawrence, the chain-smoking commander I had met operating the first Ironclad, took the controls himself. He professed to be unwilling to risk his men to the unknown dangers, though I thought perhaps he acted out of guilt that he had been unable to help his former crew. The new Ironclad had gained a great deal of weight with the addition of the reactor, necessitating the removal of the original artillery barrel along with the magazine that served it. In addition, there were now no auxiliary guns, the sole weapon being the heat ray. The projector for this perched precariously atop the turret, but the increased elevation would allow free firing in all directions and improved visibility for the operator.

Despite the removal of so much of the original vehicle's weight, the treads still sank deeper into the soft earth than before and churned it up into a quagmire, flinging foul-scented clods of earth over anyone who ventured too close. As it trundled slowly over the testing field, the projector held a steady aim, being balanced upon gimbals in a way that the original gun could not have been. Russell designated a tree as the first target, and after a few calibration firings, it delighted all assembled to see first smoke and then flame rising, before the sap boiled inside the trunk of the pine, cracking it in two. They took the rest of the afternoon up with drills for the Ironclad crew, learning to fire while in motion and improve their aim until sunset put a stop to matters.

"I wish we could use that remote piloting system," Chambers opined over dinner.

"With the radio problems all around us, it won't work," Russell replied with a mouthful of corned beef. "And it was no use for the aircraft, either. It was too tricky to fly as it was, the pilot insisted he needed to feel it moving under him to do his job. Besides, I want a reliable weapon, and that means men."

"How does your search for another reactor-man proceed?" I asked.

He shook his head. "After seeing what happened to that traitor and losing the last Ironclad, there are no volunteers. For now that falls to me."

───────◄O►───────

The following morning dawned with greater optimism, the success of the first Ironclad tests having put a spring into everyone's step. With a virtually limitless supply of power, we could test the heat ray repeatedly, and they carried out several experiments to determine the optimal distance for maximum damage, as well as the greatest practical range at which the weapon was effective. Before too long, an entire grove of trees beyond the camp fence was ablaze, billowing white smoke rising over the countryside.

Whether curious at the source of the smoke, or just wanting to put a stop to our experimentation before we could declare success, a Martian fighting machine appeared over the Northern horizon later that day. By chance, the Ironclad was fuelled up and about to start another test when the warning sounded, and we could press it into action immediately.

The *Cooper* surged at its maximum speed towards the adversary, rooster-tails of mud flying in its wake. For all the noise and mess it created, the top speed was barely more than a brisk walking pace, and we all held our breath as it covered the distance towards the Martian. I was acutely aware of how close they had to come to threaten the fighting machine, and how vulnerable they would be to a counter-attack when it came.

My concern was that the Martian would simply attack it on sight, having been informed of the danger by its compatriots. The entire camp held its breath, waiting for the first signs of it deploying its own weapon, but it foolishly allowed the machine within range, scrutinising it closely. When the heat ray fired from our makeshift platform, it came as a complete surprise.

At first it recoiled, presumably as the creature inside the carapace reacted instinctively, but then its tentacles emerged from the body. One of these groped for its own projector while the rest of them swung around wildly. The gunner on our Ironclad held his nerve, and focused the beam of the ray on these appendages, softening and melting their material and rendering them useless. Fortunately, I had been correct that the shield protected against physical damage and not heat. Unable to aim its own weapon, the Martian turned to run, but another well-aimed blast weakened one of its legs, and the tripod toppled heavily to the ground. Before the creature within had any opportunity to react further, a follow-up blast from the Ironclad left the entire machine in flames. Acrid black smoke drifted across the fields, and the crew of the Ironclad emerged to savour their victory. Cheers echoed throughout the camp, teary-eyed men and women hugging one another and celebrating. The sense of relief among us all was palpable, I for one felt a tightness in my chest that I had barely recognised begin to lift. Chambers was more sanguine, aware of the challenges we had still to face. The two fallen tripods furnished us with little information about the Martians, the fighting having extensively damaged them both. Russell, as expected, was downcast at the loss of yet another valuable piece of enemy materiel, and grumbled to any who would listen about the waste of intelligence.

That evening a previously secret stash of rum appeared, and every man and woman there had a tot. Someone produced a fiddle from somewhere, someone else improvised a drum from a water barrel, and the camp enjoyed a knees-up while the last streamers of smoke roiled in the setting sun.

Chapter Nineteen

Malaise

T he euphoria induced by the success of our attack lasted a few short days before the reality of our situation reasserted itself. We remained prisoners in our camp in all but name, as we expected that at any moment another fighting machine might crest the horizon and launch its own retaliation. We kept the watchtowers constantly manned and the Ironclad *Cooper* on standby, ready to surge forth at a moment's notice. But despite the ever-present fear of attack, it was remarkable how quickly people turned from anxiety to boredom, and then discontent. The reality of our situation weighed heavily upon us. Concerns for loved ones grew, and the confinement took its toll. Tempers frayed, and I gazed out beyond the fences and dreamed of talking a walk through the woods. I was not alone in this wanderlust; more than a few of the camp's inhabitants were spotted sneaking through holes in the fence at dawn and dusk.

Those with clear duties to perform fared best; the soldiers took turns going out on patrol, and the cooks kept inventing new concoctions to feed us (with varying levels of success). With a purpose, the mind was occupied, and not left idle to speculate about 'what next' or to perceive an insult in the strange manner of another.

Among those not otherwise distracted, fights erupted with alarming frequency. Arguments over food occurred at every mealtime, despite the plentiful supplies. Once I had to intervene in a dispute that got out of hand, with one man accusing another of moving some of his belongings inside their shared accommodation and the pair almost coming to blows. The infirmary was constantly dealing with minor injuries caused by these violent disagreements. In addition, trivial complaints swamped them, the kind that would normally be allowed to heal on its own now focused the attention when nothing else exists to form a distraction. We performed a veritable concert of sniffles and coughs daily, and a variety of ailments both real and imagined took up the medical staff's time.

Among Chambers, Russell and myself debate was vigorous about how best to capitalise on the opportunity our victory presented, but for once we were all able to find ourselves in agreement with no mediation.

We required more reactors. That much was clear — every idea we devised for how to defeat the Martians depended on piercing their shielding, and while explosives had proved able to do so, the necessity of laying a trap for a Martian rendered this unlikely to succeed. With reactors we could have heat-rays and flying machines, assuming we possessed the other materials to build them with. While the fallen fighting machines provided little in the way of information about the Martians, they supplied much of the strange metal alloy used by the invaders for our own experimentation and use. I convinced Russell to turn his attention away from the Martian technology that so interested him, at least until we found something concrete to examine, and focus on smelting and forging the physical remains of the fighting machines. Each comprised an alloy we on Earth had not yet developed. If we could master the working of it, it might well prove useful — perhaps more resilient to attacks than the steel we currently used (although we had just proven that it was not impervious to the heat ray).

To that end, I proposed a work programme, something that would both give purpose to our days and advance the efforts in which we were all engaged. To my delight, both men agreed that this solved both of our problems, occupying the under-worked members of our camp and engaging them on a useful task.

Of course, we lacked the giant industrial equipment usually required for smelting ore into steel, and working it on a vast scale. And so the ancient art of blacksmithing returned to vogue in our camp. Throughout the day, the place rang with the fall of hammers beating metal into shape, men forging tools for other men to use, and experimenting with the strange metal from Mars. Along with this activity came the need for charcoal to fuel the forges. Accordingly, pits were dug, filled with wood and lit before being covered with soil and turf to keep the air out. Wisps of smoke from the mounds scattered around the camp caused eyes to sting and coughs to develop if one lingered nearby for too long.

We made one fortunate discovery early on, and that was that the red weed was ideal for fuelling this conversion process, allowing us to leave the surrounding woodlands untouched. The moisture-laden leaves required drying out first, but the stems and roots burned wonderfully. Such was the weed's persistence that someone could harvest it almost as quickly as it grew, and the blacksmiths added sickles to their inventory of tools to ensure our supply. There was no shortage of volunteers to leave the camp and cut back the weeds, or shuttle them back to the camp for burning. Excess heat from the smelting process sped up the drying of the leaves, and productivity ramped up. Fear of the effects of burning so much of the weed on our lungs led to the pits being repositioned where the prevailing winds carried the smoke away.

Not being suited by nature to the mechanical arts, my own experiments with the noxious weed were my chosen escape from the routine. I had had little opportunity to study during the first invasion, and the weed had rotted rapidly, even the specimens kept under alcohol being degraded to the point of uselessness. Compared to my lovely roses, or the vegetables that replaced them, this was a remarkably easy plant to cultivate — a cutting sprouted roots within an hour if placed in water or damp soil — if a truly ugly example of nature's resourcefulness. But my goal was not to populate a garden with the stuff, nor to trim it into fascinating and artful shapes, but to work on a method of stifling its growth.

I did not delude myself that I would find anything remarkable, or that I would stumble across some valuable insight that would elude Russell's team of botanical experts, but my curiosity would not be sated by the spotty and fragmentary reports I received of their own researches through the official channels. So I gathered old jars from the canteen to serve as pots for the weed and placed cuttings in with a variety of local flora to see if there was any interaction. I tried slaking the soil with lime, or with potash, and even cadged some vinegar from the canteen to try adjusting the acidity of the soil. I wrote copious notes about the growth rates, documented any changes in appearance and logged the weight of the plant after various periods in a notebook. It seemed to do best in acidic soil, but its growth was only barely slowed in a soil so alkali as to be untenable for earthly life.

I tried pesticides, herbicides, fungicides: none of them had any effect. Oddly, nor did the fertilisers I tried. This led me down an unproductive avenue when I tried to nourish the local plants so well as to outgrow the invader, to little effect. It seemed able to gather the nourishment from the soil so efficiently that it left nothing of consequence for any other life.

These results were confirmed by the research team at Russell's remote site. I had pressed my courier friends into service to relay messages to them, along with my regular missives to Amy. Where her replies were brief and only confirmed that she was 'well, and busy, and do not worry', theirs were more detailed. It seems that Russell only wanted to hear from them when they had a solution to the 'red weed problem', and they relished the opportunity to share more depth of their findings with an interested amateur instead of another expert.

One thing that we both agreed on was that the bacteria which had previously stifled the growth of the weed were much less effective, if not downright useless, against the plant this time around. During the first invasion, the plant had died a few weeks after arrival, as had the Martians. This time it was still growing as rapidly and vibrantly as before, even after two weeks had passed. I had even less understanding of microbiology than I did of botany, but had attempted to grow cultures of various germs I had harvested from around the camp. While the red weed flourished in the jars I had collected, my hope for its destruction grew in the upturned lids I had pressed into use as culture plates. These unfortunately emitted foul stenches as they progressed, and my neighbours complained that the scents wafting under my door were unacceptable. I poured the cultures over my weed samples, and placed them on the window-sill outside, hoping one of them might prove deadly.

None did. I reported this to my new botanist friends, and they confirmed they had met with a similar lack of success. I had found a couple of strains which they had not, and was glad to have made some small contribution to our knowledge, however negative, but they had access to many more samples than I did. In fact, they boasted they had caches of some of the nastiest diseases known to man to experiment with, and that if typhoid, tuberculosis and syphilis could not slow the advance of the weed, nothing I found in the bathrooms of our camp was likely to have much effect either.

After this last exchange, however, their communication dwindled. At first I thought someone had instructed them to cease cooperating with me, but I could extract from one that most of their scientists had been engaged on another project at Russell's direct request. I could see nothing that would be of more importance than securing our future food supplies against the weed, and confronted him.

When I tracked the man down, he appeared annoyed that I had even heard anything about some other project, and refused to engage with me about it. Nevertheless I pressed him.

"I can only assume it's to defeat the Martians, since that's the only thing I can imagine being more important than securing our food supply. And we've not seen that air purifier you lifted from the cylinder since that day, so I presume that's related." Russell shifted uneasily. "So you're looking for something to interfere with their air supply, perhaps to stop the purifier working... no, they'd spot that immediately and remedy it. You intend to bypass it!"

"Oh, very clever," he snapped.

"And since your chemists aren't involved, but rather the biologists..." I understood the idea now. "You mean to get our bacteria back into their systems again?"

Despite his annoyance, he was clearly proud of his work. "Not just the mundane ones we carry about every day, but a new strain, one that acts faster still. Besides, the Martians probably have medicines or vaccines against what they saw last time, we have to step up our game."

"You've been breeding germs to use against them?" I gasped.

"They reproduce so quickly, those little germs, and pass on their traits nice and fast. Whenever we put them in a difficult environment, most of them die, of course, but those that are hardy enough to survive pass on that strength. A few generations, just a few days, and we change their conditions. Repeat that for just a few weeks and we have something dashed hard to shake off. The Martians won't stand a chance!"

Chapter Twenty

Destruction

I did not share Russell's enthusiasm for this approach, nor his confidence in its efficacy. "Might it not turn on us, too?" I worried. "You might unleash some demon upon mankind, and doom us along with the Martians!"

"Nonsense," he scoffed. "Desperate times require equally desperate measures. And besides, all this work is being performed in a separate location, so the risk to ourselves is minimal."

Amy. She had sought shelter at the same place Russell was now endangering. I resolved to send her a message as soon as I could.

"And the couriers?" I asked. "They may bring you more than reports on your new weapon, you realise. An infection like that would decimate us."

"Precautions are being taken," he dismissed my concerns with a wave of his hand. "You act as if we do not understand what we are doing."

"I fear you do not," I replied. "It is not so long since the prevailing wisdom was that disease was caused by a foul scent, or stale air, or..."

"Our advancements are many, and remarkable, since those dark days," Russell countered. "Have you so little faith..."

A loud whistle from the observation tower interrupted him.

Russell and I glared at each other for a moment, and then bolted from the room. We arrived moments later in the courtyard, where we found a large crowd milling around aimlessly, unable to see anything over the gates and fences, and arguing among themselves about what had caused the alarm. A low grinding and rumbling sound came from behind us, and the Ironclad *Cooper* hauled itself into view, flanked by a company of soldiers brandishing rifles and mortars.

Since my last sighting of our great defender, it had undergone some alterations. They had affixed panels of the strange Martian metal all over it, lending it a patchwork appearance. Cracks where the pieces did not quite meet squarely broke the dull shine of the oddly shaped and rough-beaten shapes, and allowed a glimpse of the original structure underneath. The added armour was suspended a couple of inches from the surface of the machine, giving it a bulkier and altogether even more menacing air than it had previously exuded.

It was also slower moving. Despite its sturdier appearance, this left me fearing for its vulnerability. Would it be able to outmanoeuvre any Martian attack, or even get itself into position to strike without being destroyed? Russell raced after it, catching it quickly and hauling himself on top of the body. He stood, almost pitching himself into the treads of the machine, before regaining his footing and clambering inside to run the reactor, slamming the hatch behind him.

The crowd was staring at the upgraded Ironclad with a mixture of disbelief and confusion, and some soldiers escorting it pushed people aside to clear a route for the behemoth, before they could open the gates and surge out into positions. The Ironclad followed them out at a frighteningly sedate pace.

Before the gates closed behind it, we all had a clear view of a silhouette on the horizon, a large fighting machine outlined in profile. Even without binoculars, I could see it clearly. To my eye, it appeared larger than its brethren. I hoped it was a trick of the view, that it was actually just closer than I suspected and not some newer, more dangerous variant.

I spotted Chambers climbing the stairs to the observation tower two at a time and set off after him. There we met the lookout who informed us that my assessment had been accurate. This was a new, larger tripod.

"Not taller, but the body is longer and wider than the last, the legs sturdier and it moves faster."

Chambers' lips drew tight before he spoke. "Fortunately, you spotted it early, and we have a chance. Well done." He lifted his binoculars, and I did likewise.

The Ironclad was running at full tilt towards the new arrival, hoping to head it off before it came within range of our encampment. As the distance increased, the speed appeared to slow, until I was unsure it was even moving above a man's walking pace.

"How far can it reach?" I asked. "What's the range of the heat-ray?"

Chambers shrugged. "My worry is that this new model has a larger ray, and thus a longer range. It might even have a bigger reactor. We could well be outmatched here."

The soldiers outside the camp had advanced slowly behind the Ironclad and now deployed themselves on either side of the road. Orders were given, rendered inaudible to us by the distance and the still loud grumbling of the vehicle, and the mortar teams readied their weapons.

Synchronised puffs of smoke told me they had fired, and twin impacts spurted part-way between the Ironclad and the Martian. Moments later, those spots vanished behind thick white smoke, which quickly covered the entire road. It clung strangely to the ground, resisting the light breeze that ruffled my hair in the tower. Was it specially engineered to do that, or was it just a freak still spot in the air? Whichever it was, the Ironclad advanced upon it relentlessly before diving into the cloud and vanishing from sight. Only the rattling sound of the Ironclad's engine reassured me it had not disappeared from the Earth entirely.

The Martian stopped its own advance, evidently confused or curious about this new tactic, and unable to bring its own weapons to bear on an unseen enemy. I gave a silent prayer of thanks to whoever had devised this smoke for buying the safety of Lawrence, Russell and their men.

Then the fighting machine deployed its grasping tentacles, waving them around as if trying to fan the smoke away. This had no effect, the smoke being too distant to be affected by such a minimal disturbance. The creature within the tripod must have realised this at the same moment I did, as one tentacle reached inside the carapace and pulled out something resembling a barrel with a pipe attached. It aimed this towards the smoke, and a scalding jet of steam issued forth. Where the cloud came into contact with this spray, it dissipated, and the Martian directed the steam in a series of wide, sweeping arcs to disperse the Ironclad's cover.

Silence descended over the tower as we all held our breath to see what would happen next. The only sounds were the low noise of the Ironclad's engine in the distance, and the voice of a man relaying news to the crowd beneath. As the cloud of smoke retreated in the face of the Martian's steam, I let out an involuntary cry as the Ironclad emerged from its concealment barely a hundred yards from the fighting machine. It began jinking around, hoping to avoid coming under fire. The Martian now fumbled the steam-spray back into his carapace and swiftly had his heat-ray at the ready, following the movements of its prey as best it could. It did not fire immediately, perhaps waiting for a clear shot. I watched our Ironclad slow, pivot sharply and take position behind a few shrubs and low bracken. This would not offer it any protection or even any concealment, so I couldn't see why Lawrence had selected that position.

The Martian stepped closer, and its heat-ray stabbed at the Ironclad. Instantly flames consumed the shrubs and foliage, and the external shell of the land-ship glowed a dull cherry-red. The burning vegetation emitted vast clouds of smoke and hid the scene from view momentarily. A moment later, the sound of a low explosion reached us.

"The Ironclad!" I gasped, but Chambers motioned me to calm myself. As the smoke cleared, I saw that the Martian's leg was scorched and damaged, a claymore hidden in the shrubs used to try to cripple it. The Ironclad, its outer protective layer still glowing red but clearly unharmed, spun the turret to face the injured leg. The heat-ray focused on this spot and bored through the metal, causing the Martian to sway and topple. It smacked into the ground, sending skyward a shower of earth, and I waited for the killing blow to be delivered.

Instead, the *Cooper* circled slowly around the fallen machine, always keeping its ray trained upon it, but never firing. The whole time it was cooling from a dull red to black, though a shimmering heat-haze above it told us that the Martian metal was still hot enough to burn a man. Once it was in position behind the carapace, the hatch on top opened up. Water cascaded down the sides of the vehicle, sizzling into steam at first, before it sapped away the heat. Once this was done, the men inside streamed out and levelled their rifles at the machine. The soldiers who had accompanied the Ironclad out of the gates had also moved up into position and encircled the fallen enemy. Russell climbed down after them all and took position behind the largest of the soldiers.

"Come on," Chambers muttered under his breath. "Come on out, damn you."

"You mean to capture the creature within?" I asked, incredulously.

"I'm more interested in the equipment, this appears to be the first of a new type of machine. But if the Martian survived, we can deal with him right enough. Come on, let's go."

As we dashed over to the scene, I had to wonder if Russell had put him up to this, somehow won over his suspicions. What deals might have the two men have brokered while I was otherwise distracted? When we arrived, Chambers took charge for once, issuing orders to the men surrounding the downed machine. Having evidently decided its pilot was dead, they moved in. Two of them forced open the hatch, and checked inside with periscopes, rather than expose themselves to danger, but pronounced the coast clear. I stepped forward with Chambers and Russell, and together we peered inside.

<hr />

The interior of the Martian fighting machine was darker than I expected. No light came from the screens which served as substitutes for windows, and only the dim glow of the other instruments and a strip of light across the ceiling illuminated the place. These lights were a pale yellow-orange, dim to suit the eyes of a creature which evolved on a planet further from the life-giving sun. The equipment and apparatus inside shared the reddish hue of the creature's home planet, which cast an eerie air over the scene — I could almost imagine myself on the surface of Mars. The impression I had previously had within the destroyed cylinder, of being surrounded by blood-soaked walls, returned, and I shuddered. A cloying, metallic smell pervaded the space, and I realised I had neglected to put on my gas mask. Hurriedly donning it, hoping I had not exposed myself to danger, I peered about for the source of the scent. As my eyes grew accustomed to the gloom, I saw it.

The creature itself was dead, sure enough. When the machine fell it had clearly knocked its head (or what passed for it) and a thick sticky blood had pooled black beneath it. Russell clambered in, keen to investigate deeper, but something held me back. Was I squeamish to see one of these beasts up close again? Reluctantly, I followed, bent double under the low roof. I was careful to avoid the former occupant and turned my back on it to examine the controls of the fighting machine.

I could barely make sense of them. There were altogether too many of them to comprehend, and even the function of most of them was obscure to me. I thought back to the disassembled machine I had seen in London, and realised that this one was more complex, and more advanced than that one had been. I looked for similarities, assuming that there would be some continuity of purpose within the design, and I might glean some information.

I focused on the instruments and levers closest to the view-ports. The most vital controls would be there, I reasoned, in easy reach of the pilot. Three larger levers protruded from a forest of smaller ones, and I decided that these would be the means by which the legs were moved and operated. I reached out towards them, but a voice behind me halted my hand.

"Better not," Chambers said. "We've a dozen or more trigger-happy men outside and if this thing starts twitching, they're likely to shoot anyone or anything they see."

I snatched my hand back quickly. "Do you know how it works?" I asked him. Chambers had probably spent more time with these devices than any other man.

He nodded. "Those larger levers control the legs, but they're extremely sensitive. Driving this thing is more of an art than anything. We tried some tests with our captive suspended from a crane, but we could never do more than just flail about. Locomotion was well beyond our abilities."

"And these others?" I pointed at the shorter levers surrounding the longer ones. They looked disturbingly organic, as if they might start wriggling by themselves at any moment.

"Tentacles," Chambers replied simply. "The handling apparatus is controlled through those."

"I can't imagine anyone mastering that," I said. "Even a concert pianist would struggle with the level of coordination that must be required."

"Ah, but they have a hand for each one, you see?" Chambers crawled over to the corpse in the middle of the control room. To my horror, he grabbed a tentacle that bordered the lipless mouth and tugged on it. It extended smoothly to over five feet in length before he released it and it slowly retracted to its former size. "More dextrous than the octopus, and quite delicate, we believe. We might better consider them as tongues, rather than hands."

Despite my disgust for the beast, the idea fascinated me. I crawled over on hands and knees and regarded the Martian from a few feet away. I imagined I could still smell the metallic scent of its blood despite my mask, and I worked to breathe as little as possible. The vast eyes I remembered from my first encounter as jet-black pools had turned a milky white, but were no less disturbing to behold. I had read treatises on the physiology of the Martians after the first invasion, but had never seen one this close up. I took a deep breath and endeavoured to focus on the scientific aspects of the situation.

"I thought so!" came a triumphant cry from the rear of the cabin, causing me to jump and bash my head. Russell's head reappeared from the gloom and he bore a wide grin. "Come and see!"

Rubbing the lump on my head and swallowing one in my throat, I climbed over the sill of the door, gave the occupant of the craft a wide berth and followed his voice to the rear of the cabin. He was pointing a torch at some instruments and still grinning.

"What is it?" I asked.

"The reactor!" he replied. "This larger machine has a new reactor inside! It is smaller than ours, but must be no less powerful. More advanced too, perhaps, but either way we have another one now. And if it's lighter and smaller, that gives us flexibility."

Chapter Twenty-One

Prepare

It took most of a day and night to extract that reactor, with men working in the confined space amidst the ever-present risk of a leak of the fatal energies within. No-one could relax until they had safely secured the device in the workshops. More of the Martian alloy salvaged from the fallen tripod was beaten into heavy plating shields which were arranged around it, despite Russell's assurances that the unit itself was perfectly safe to handle.

Any agreement that might have existed between Chambers and Russell evaporated the moment they had control of the power source. The two men fought the entire time about the best use for the reactor, debating the relative merits of another heat-ray, a flying machine, or in their wildest moments speculating that the lighter reactor might enable some combination of the two. While I agreed that an airborne heat-ray would indeed prove wonderfully effective, I had to urge them to caution.

"We have no certainty yet that the new, smaller reactor is still as powerful as the previous one, and whether that would prove sufficient to power both flight and weaponry," I reminded them.

"My men are confident it's at least as effective, if not more so," Russell explained. "They're running more tests now to confirm it. We must press it into service."

"Even if it were, we have no working airframe, and I fear it is unlikely we shall have time to prepare one before another attack comes."

"We have a better source of material now," Russell retorted. "The Martian mineral is lighter and stronger than steel, and an airframe composed of that could carry greater loads even without a smaller reactor."

"I know," Chambers replied. "But the truth of the matter is that we might have only a day or two before the next Martian returns, or more than one. We have proven ourselves a threat to them now, and I cannot believe for one moment that they will let us complete all but the hastiest preparations."

In the end, practical necessity dictated that the new power source be used to power the heat-ray on the Ironclad *Cooper*, something even Russell had to agree was valuable. Being lighter, it would allow the vehicle to move more rapidly and react more quickly than it had done during its last attack. The original, larger reactor would power the static heat-ray at the camp, affording those people within some measure of protection once more. The blacksmiths forged more shielding plates from the fallen tripod for this purpose, to protect any operator from danger.

In a remarkable stroke of luck, Chamber's fears of a rapid attack had been pessimistic. While we continued this recent work, guards kept a careful watch for more Martian activity, but whether through fear of our new capabilities or a lack of fighting machines in the area, we saw none. An unexpected side-effect of this was that the radios began working again. We now had communication with field agents up to twenty miles away, though beyond that range the Martian interference still held sway.

To our collective surprise, some of these brave souls were still alive, hiding in harm's way against the hope that they would regain contact with us one day. Their reports, carefully noted down day by day, allowed us to piece together the movement of the Martians over the period. While Russell focused on preparing the Ironclad once more, Chambers and I pored over maps of the local area, cross-referencing report after report with the location of the scout until my dreams were a confusion of grid references and elevations.

Eventually we determined that there was most likely a Martian base of operations around thirty-five miles North-West of us, to which we dispatched two nearer scouts. The hours waiting for their report tested my patience to the limit. I wished I could call them up, ask for a report, but Chambers correctly pointed out that the radio equipment would be turned off to avoid detection, so they would not hear our call. The only thing to do was to wait, gnaw on my fingernails, and issue a silent prayer to whoever might be watching over our intrepid field scouts.

Just as I was about to give up hope that they had evaded capture, a report came in. There was indeed a centre of activity near the town of Wrexham. Just outside a small wood was a hollow in the ground to which several cylinders had been brought by the invaders. Fighting machines came and went at all hours to replenish supplies and do who-knows-what else.

There was also a prison camp.

The scouts hadn't managed a precise count of the occupants, but it was clear from the size of it that many thousands of people had been taken there. From the previous invasion, I could only imagine that they would become a food source for the Martians, if they had solved the problems of infection. Some small part of me hoped they would never resolve that issue, and we might rescue our fellow men.

This news excited all of us, Russell most of all.

"If we can strike a blow at their local HQ, we might buy ourselves some breathing space," he said. For once Chambers and I agreed with him, and we set to work planning the assault.

━━◆◇◆━━

With our new flow of information from the soldiers in the field, we could keep better tabs on the movement of the Martians, which reduced the levels of anxiety felt within the camp. Knowing that there is not about to be a fighting machine looming over the fences allowed us all to sleep better at night.

Chambers and Russell worked together more comfortably, too. Their regular arguments became less frequent, and less heated when they did eventually come to a head. I was no longer occupied with refereeing their disputes, which gave me more time to dwell on other matters.

I wished I could discuss these recent developments with Amy. Our remote site was informed of the news, but so far I had received no word from her. The couriers frequently reassured me that all was well, but could not enlighten me how she was truly feeling, what her daily activities were or even how she felt towards me. The absence of a personal message, of course, revealed much about this last concern. I would lie await at night wondering if she was doing the same, unwilling to consider that she might not spare me much thought at all.

The upgrades to the Ironclad occupied Russell more often than not. Along with Lawrence, who would command it, I usually found him in the workshop sheds overseeing the work and discussing the benefits and drawbacks of any changes with the foreman of the mechanics. When possible, Lawrence also assisted Chambers with planning the assault. I knew which of the men he was visiting by the harsh scent of his tobacco, usually detectable at some distance. His expertise was invaluable, as might be expected. He was the man with the most experience of the Ironclads, and along with his crew, had the best understanding of what its capabilities in the field truly were. We debated plan after plan and dismissed the majority. Some were untenable because the terrain would not be suitable for the machine to traverse, or would leave it too exposed, or at risk of bogging down. Without his knowledge and perseverance, I doubt we would even come close to the Martian base of operations.

While Chambers planned the assault with Lawrence, I attempted to keep myself busy by updating the maps with the location and movements of the Martians. I discovered an aptitude for determining patterns in the comings and goings, and could soon piece together a reasonable estimate of the enemy's patrol routes from the sporadic sighting reports that came in to us.

Before too long, we had a workable battle plan ready to implement. There was a gap in the Martian surveillance that we could slip the Ironclad through, and a choice of locations for it to lie in wait while we assembled the assaulting forces. Russell dispatched the field operatives to reconnoitre the locations, and report back. To their absolute credit, every one of them marched into danger without a protest. Of the five who left, four sent reports back, and only two escaped alive.

Their sacrifice would not be in vain. We felt we had planned for every conceivable contingency, addressed every avenue of retreat for the Martians, and prepared against every potential pitfall. There was no shortage of volunteers either — every man there was keen to strike back at the invaders, and the recent successes had bolstered the optimism we all shared. So many soldiers wished to accompany the mission that lots needed to be drawn to select those who would take part.

———————◄O►———————

As the plans for the assault came together, Russell and Chambers each tried to win me over to their way of thinking. Russell, naturally, focused on the military objective of destroying the Martian base and rendering them unable to strike back at us, at least for some time. Chambers prioritised the rescue of the civilians trapped in the camp. When the plan had only existed in a nebulous form, they had agreed easily on the details. Now, the night before the planned attack, movements on the ground were being plotted. I feared their disagreements would come to a head once more.

But for once, they did not need me to spell out the obvious compromise.

"Two forces," Russell explained, "one takes down the Martians, and then the other comes in to liberate the civilians."

"Shouldn't we free them first?" Chambers asked. "Get them out of the line of fire?"

Russell took a deep breath before responding. "If we fling open the camp gates, the Martians will follow. The civilians will die, and we'll never be able to chase down the fighting machines. Risky as it is, we have to do it this way."

I didn't like the idea of fighting the Martians so close to the prisoners, but had to admit he was correct. And I noted that for once he had calmly stated the reasons for his decision, rather than trying to pull rank.

While the crew filled the Ironclad's fuel tanks with diesel, Lawrence and Chambers checked over the route one last time. I pointed out the Martian patrol routes, unchanged as confirmed by radio from the observers in the field just that morning. Lawrence made some marks with a grease pencil on his own copy of the map as we talked.

"I don't want to bother you, while we're busy," he explained with a smile, lighting a cigarette from the lantern illuminating the map.

"And we don't know if radio will still work at that range, and at that time," I added. I got puzzled looks from all sides.

"Why would we need to radio you?" Chambers asked.

It was my turn to be confused. "Why, I should be too far away to be heard otherwise!"

"You're not joining us?" Russell asked. "Why not?"

Of all the people I might have expected to want me alongside them, Russell was the last. "Why would I walk into battle? I offered no help last time."

"Nonsense," Chambers retorted. "We should not have got this far without you. Who else would keep Russell and I from each other's throats?" His tone was light, but he was not entirely joking. "This battle is as much yours as it is anyone's."

"I consider you a good luck charm," Russell added.

I knew what Amy would say. What she had said, in fact, the last time I had proposed such a risky endeavour. I knew that a war was no place for a writer, least of all one still scarred from his last encounters. I knew they did not truly need my talents in the field, that even Chambers and Russell could refrain from murdering one another when the cause required it. And I knew they would all fare just as well, if not better, without needing to worry if I were safe.

"Tell me all about it when you get back," I said.

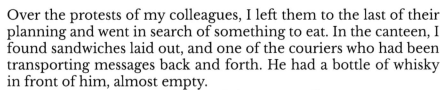

Over the protests of my colleagues, I left them to the last of their planning and went in search of something to eat. In the canteen, I found sandwiches laid out, and one of the couriers who had been transporting messages back and forth. He had a bottle of whisky in front of him, almost empty.

"Davies, isn't it?" I asked. "Mind if I join you?"

He shifted awkwardly before nodding. "Ready for the off?" he asked, his words slightly slurred. How much of the bottle had he drunk?

"I think they're prepared," I replied. "But I'm glad I ran into you. I wanted to thank you again for bringing me news of my wife."

"It's nothing," he mumbled, avoiding my eyes.

"On the contrary. Just knowing she is safe and well is a tremendous relief to me. I can't imagine how I'd have coped without that."

Davies hunched over his empty glass, and his shoulders shook. Was he crying? He tried to speak, but his sobbing jumbled and broke his words.

I placed a hand on his shoulder. "Look at me," I urged him.

He looked up, eyes brimming.

"What's the matter?" I asked.

"It's all lies!" he shouted.

Chapter Twenty-Two

Discovery

"What do you mean?" I asked. "Who is lying, and about what?"

Tears rolled down Davies' cheeks. He looked me square in the eyes for the first time. "Russell. He knows. He's known for days. He tells us what we can, and what we can't..." he trailed off into sobs.

"Knows what, man?" I grabbed his arm and shook him. "What is going on?"

"The Martians raided the camp. Captured almost everyone, scattered the rest. They might even know about our plans, our bacteria, everything." He spoke quietly, slurring his words slightly, but he might as well have shouted, so deeply did his words strike me. "And he won't let us tell... I couldn't tell you..."

"Tell me what?" I asked, my stomach sinking.

"Your poor wife."

"Ah, I thought you'd reconsider," Russell said, smiling as I strode over towards the planning table. My fist crunched into his face with all the pent-up fear and worry I had felt since Amy left, and his nose crunched beneath the blow. He reeled back, grabbed at his bloodied face, and fell to the floor in shock.

"You knew!" I bellowed, spit flying from my mouth. "You knew, for five days you knew and you didn't tell me!"

Chambers stood open-mouthed, unsure whether to help Russell to his feet or restrain me.

"Bloody Davies," Russell mumbled behind his hand. "Drunken idiot."

I kicked him. "The camp raided, everyone taken, and this... this lunatic thought it better if we didn't know!"

Chambers rounded on him. "Is this true? They're the prisoners, your own men?"

"And my wife!" I shouted. "Taken along with the others, to have who knows what happen to her! I should kill you here and now!"

"What possible reason could you have for keeping this from us?" Chambers asked.

"Security," Russell pulled himself to his feet using the table. "We know there are those who sympathise with the Martians. I felt it prudent..."

"You think I am one of them? After everything I have seen and done, you believe I would betray humanity to those... beasts?" In that moment, I would have handed him over without a second thought, watched with pleasure as they tore him limb from limb.

Chambers led me away, no doubt concerned I might do something rash. I cast one last look over my shoulder at Russell, wiping the blood from his face.

"How could he?" I was still shaking, the anger and hatred coursing through me like fire. Chambers had brought me back to the canteen, where Davies had now gone, his bottle empty. "I had a right to know!"

"And what would you have done if you had?" Chambers pressed a mug of hot, sweet tea into my hand. "Worried about her, feared for her, of course. And probably set out to rescue her single-handedly, against all our better judgement."

His words hit close to the mark. I had been trying to work out how to rescue Amy from the moment I had learned of her fate. "So you think he did the right thing?" I asked. Tea slopped over my hand as I shook, and I dropped the mug. It shattered on the floor and I wiped my scalded hand on my shirt.

"I won't defend him, or his actions," Chambers said. "But if it kept you from running off into the night to die pointlessly, then I can be grateful for that at least."

"What now?" I asked.

"We have a plan. Whoever the prisoners are makes no difference to that, or to the objective." He held up his hands in supplication. "I know, it makes a difference to you, of course it does. But nothing changes for the volunteers tomorrow morning, nor the crew of the *Cooper*."

"I'm coming." The words left my mouth without me realising.

Chambers nodded. "I rather thought you might."

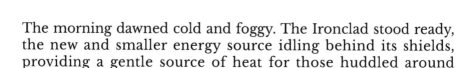

The morning dawned cold and foggy. The Ironclad stood ready, the new and smaller energy source idling behind its shields, providing a gentle source of heat for those huddled around beside it. I worried at first that more dangerous emanations would accompany this heat, but Chambers explained I was safe.

"That is radiation of a very different kind," he explained. "The shields trap and contain the danger, but even they must eventually heat up. I assure you: you could sit directly atop them and suffer nothing more than perspiration!"

I kept a prudent distance from the Ironclad and trusted in my hat and gloves to insulate me against the weather.

Russell had a black and purple bruise spreading across his face, and his right eye had almost swollen shut. He had the sense to keep away from me, and for my part, I tried not to smile at his disfigurement.

With all the preparations completed, it was time to embark. I climbed up into the rear of the truck where Chambers and Russell sat on bench seating bolted to the sides. Opposite them were a handful of soldiers, and I asked one of them if I might have his seat. I wanted to be at the rear, nearest the fresh air, to avoid feeling nauseous again.

"Give him your seat, Mitchell," Sergeant Webb ordered, and a pimply faced youth grudgingly stood and walked to the front of the truck bed, where he sat down cross-legged between his comrades' feet. Between the two benches, strapped down to the centre of the truck floor, were barrels of diesel fuel, additional ammunition supplies, food and water.

The engine fired up, and we set off through the gates. Another truck swung in behind us, and the Ironclad took up the rear position.

The soldiers busied themselves checking and rechecking their weapons in between sharing bawdy jokes with one another. Our convoy would have made a curious sight, trundling through the countryside that morning. The mist still lay in the lowest hollows, and a casual observer would have seen diesel lorries alternately vanishing and reappearing as they encountered small fog banks. Most peculiar of all to their eyes would be the upgraded Ironclad. The patchwork of armour panels had a slapdash appearance, denser towards the front of the vehicle than the rear. The projector of the heat-ray stuck a short distance out from the front of it, and swung periodically from side to side as the gunner inside surveyed the surroundings. For now at least, the hatch atop the turret was open, and the upper half of Lawrence's body protruded into the chilly morning air.

"Why is the Ironclad not leading the way?" I asked, shouting to be heard over the noise of the engines. "If we run into trouble it'd be best in the vanguard, surely."

"It's the most valuable part of this whole caravan," Russell replied. "If we find trouble, then it might escape and continue the mission."

The red weed had conquered the terrain beyond our camp, and our vehicles crushed it into the dust beneath us as we proceeded. The blood-sweet smell of it grew stronger the further we went, and I fought down nausea once more. Red was the overwhelming colour of the once-familiar countryside. Few of the native plants were visible above the weed, mostly the taller trees already naked from winter's approach. Even these were being climbed by the invading flora, and would soon succumb. I saw no birds or other wildlife as we passed, and even if they had been hiding, I would never have heard any hint of them over the sound of diesel motors.

We passed through the local village, from where the protesters at our gate had come. No people lined the streets, no faces appeared at windows, no signs of occupation were to be seen. Something had cracked open or destroyed most of the houses, and I pictured the Martian fighting machines using their tentacles to break into the homes around us and pluck their occupants out. The red weed was already growing over the rubble and had made its way at least half-way up the sides of what buildings still stood. Despite the noise of the convoy, the place had an eerie feel. I shivered in a manner that had nothing to do with the cold.

As we left the dead town behind, we encountered a black mound on the outskirts. A flock of crows erupted from it, revealing it to be a pile of dead bodies in an advanced state of decay.

I gagged at the stench and coughed out a question. "Is that all of them, do you think?"

"I hope not," Chambers mumbled through his hand. "Though I wouldn't want to imagine what any survivors might be facing."

We fell into silence as our convoy passed the mass grave, and the wind brought fresher air to our noses.

Mid-morning brought a rest halt. The soldiers sprang into action the second we stopped, most of them dashing out to form a circle around us, rifles drawn and ready. Once they were in position, we disembarked, stretched our legs, and attended to any calls of nature. Russell and Chambers watched the horizon, scanning all directions for any sight of the Martians. I watched as the Ironclad's crew worked to unpack the diesel barrels, top off the tanks, and re-strap them down for safety in just a few minutes. Clearly they were well-practised, and I grudgingly had to admire the efficacy of Russell's training, though of course I would never admit it to him. Cold rations were handed out, along with water, and then we clambered back into our uncomfortable seats to resume the journey.

Despite my fears of what we would encounter, the low rumble of the engine, the gentle rocking back and forth and the early hour of our start after a sleepless night all conspired to make me drowsy. I fought sleep as long as I could, but I awoke when we stopped again, and the soldiers leapt into action. Checking my watch, I noted it was just past noon, and I stretched to relieve the crick in my neck before climbing down to see where we were.

We had drawn to a halt in a wooded area at the base of a small rise in the ground. The fresh scent of pine was welcome after the cloying odour that had accompanied most of our journey. Here we met Lloyd-Thomas, the resistance fighter with whom we had been in radio contact, and he informed us we were about a mile south of the Martian HQ. Chambers, Russell, Webb, Lawrence and I climbed the ridge with him and observed the Martians through binoculars.

The camp comprised a circle of the cylinders — I counted half a dozen — all set on end atop the earth.

"Why so many?" I wondered aloud.

"They've gathered them from all over," Russell stated. "Safety in numbers, you see."

Chambers disagreed. "That would leave the neighbouring regions undefended. More likely they're building them in situ, boosting their capabilities across the country."

"D'you see that setup behind them?" Lloyd-Thomas asked, pointing beyond the Martians. There was an area maybe a half-mile away from the encampment, separated from it by a low hill. It was surrounded by vertical stakes of the strange metal, so close together as to form a complete wall. At that distance, it was hard to judge, but they had to be at least ten feet tall. Within the corral thus formed were low structures, rough cabins and tents cobbled together from whatever materials must have been at hand. The contrast between these make-shift shelters and the Martians' own constructions was stark. At the very limit of my vision, I saw figures moving slowly around, and realised with horror that this was the prison camp.

We turned our attention back to the structures in front of us. Cables and pipes snaked between the cylinders, and a bundle of these led to a large mechanism attached to a hopper. Around the site mechanical devices roamed, evidently serving as transport or manipulation machines. As we watched, one transferred a load of excavated soil from a quarry site nearby into the hopper, from where it vanished inside some of the machinery. A plate of the strange alloy emerged from the side of one such machine, curved to the same radius as the cylinders. To Chambers' credit — and my relief — he did not comment on this, and Russell merely remained quiet in the face of his earlier theory being disproven. One of the handling machines picked the section up and manoeuvred it next to another piece, building the start of a new cylinder. Whatever mineral they had found here, we had to assume they transmuted it into something of more use to the Martians. I saw no creatures outside these contraptions, they no doubt occupied the cylinders when not engaged in work.

"It's the same schedule most days," Lloyd-Thomas said. "One o' those three-legged things comes in each hour or so from the West, refuels or re-arms for about twenty-five minutes, then leaves the same way it comes in."

"Can you be any more precise about the timings?" Russell snapped.

The fighter stared at him for a second in silence, before reaching into his breast-pocket and withdrawing a battered notebook. "Yesterday: tripod arrived 09:14, departed 09:35. Tripod arrived 10:18, departed 10:37. Tripod arrived 11:23, departed..."

"Yes, that will do," Russell said, temporarily mollified. Chambers and I exchanged a smile.

"Sounds predictable enough to work with," Chambers said. "When might we expect to see something?" He asked our new acquaintance.

"In about a half-hour."

"Let's camouflage the Ironclad just in case."

The crew had already been hard at work chopping brush and branches to cover the machine from casual inspection. From a distance it worked wonderfully, but we trusted that the Martians didn't have some way of detecting the vehicle that didn't rely on optical means. So it proved, as a few minutes after one o'clock a fighting machine strode in from the West and didn't so much as glance in our direction. Lying prone on the ground, we watched it march into the camp, position itself directly above one cylinder which had been propped upright, and slowly lower itself by shortening its legs. With a clang it came to rest, then metallic scraping sounds reached us as the smaller machines worked on connecting cables and conduits. Once they were done, a small escape of steam or air hissed around it before all was quiet again.

"Right, first target is that tripod," Russell said. "We've seen that they can't shield it when it's rearming like that. Then the cylinders, they might have some defences too. Without them we can mop up those little servicing machines. I don't see them being armed. Let's go."

"Time to split up," Chambers announced. "Good luck."

Webb led the detachment of soldiers who were going to liberate the camp, and they set off down the ridge line towards their goal. I carried the radio, so as to leave the soldiers unencumbered for the battle ahead. The leather straps it hung from dug into my shoulders, and the stiff wooden frame dug into my back with each step. I bunched up my jacket in the small of my back to try and cushion the repeated blows as it bounced. Having a job to do, however painful, gave me something to focus on. That and the need to rescue Amy were the only things driving me forwards. If she had not been in peril, I'd have been safe and warm in the map room, watching the movement of figures and biting my nails as the reports came in. But people were relying on me now. I was our contingent's point of contact with the rest of the operation, and could not let them down.

The trucks had already taken up position nearer the camp, hidden from view until the diversion took place. I followed the line of soldiers, with one last look over my shoulder. Lawrence scurried back to the Ironclad where the crew were already removing the camouflage. Chambers, Russell, Lloyd-Thomas remained behind to observe, they would stay in radio contact with the Ironclad in case of any surprises. The newer reactor was so simple to operate, the gunner was able to manage it without Russell's presence being required.

I could not help but watch as the machine trundled along, despite tripping and almost losing my footing for lack of attention.

The Ironclad kept below the ridgeline until about a half-mile West of us. It then followed the path by which the tripod had entered, and came within a few hundred yards of its objective before we saw any sign of it having been spotted.

The servicing machines reacted first — hurrying towards the refuelling fighting machine as if to cut it free from its moorings. I was about to shout a warning into the radio, but the Ironclad's heat-ray struck through the heart of the tripod before I could manage. It exploded most satisfyingly, destroying the cylinder upon which it had rested.

Now the other machines which had not been caught in the blast turned their attention upon their foe. Short staccato bursts from the machine gun didn't appear to damage them, but they withdrew slightly as the rounds ricocheted off their outer shells. Meanwhile, the heat-ray continued to slice through cylinder after cylinder, making it half-way around the circle before a loud cry of "ulla" echoed around us and was answered from every direction. From each point of the compass, a Martian fighting machine had appeared.

Chapter Twenty-Three

Rescue

"The fighting machines!" Russell's voice burst from the earpiece I wore, connected to the radio. "Take them down!"
"Let them work," I muttered to myself. "They'll take care of it."
I could not draw my eyes away from the scene, however. A single tripod had proven itself capable of destroying an Ironclad before, and even with the upgrades we had made, I was not as confident in the *Cooper's* abilities as Lawrence evidently was.

The Ironclad immediately started a zig-zagging retreat. The operator of the heat-ray swung the projector around to bear on each of the machines without firing, no doubt deciding which would be in range first. A jet of heat burst forth towards it from a larger tripod, and was quickly followed up by more. At such extreme range these barrages missed, but narrowly, and the driver of the land-ship piled on all speed. Lawrence's experience, combined with the Ironclad crew's drills and exercises, paid off. They landed a blow on the nearer Martian's foremost leg, bringing it to a halt before it collapsed to the ground, opening an exit route. The Ironclad spun and headed for the gap in the Martian lines, jinking irregularly to throw off the enemy's aim.

Another shot brought down a second fighting machine, and the crew were practically flying towards safety when we reached the low rise separating the battle from the prison camp, and lost sight of them. Reluctantly, I spun down the gain on the radio to focus on the task at hand. The rumble of the Ironclad's engine faded as we increased our distance, but still formed a backdrop to our marching.

It did not take us long to cover the intervening distance, and we encountered none of the Martians along the way. Russell's diversionary plan was evidently working, and we reached the camp in safety.

Webb's forces spread along the ground just a few hundred yards from the camp, taking cover behind a hedge that had once divided farm fields. I lay next to him, peering out through the foliage, and together we surveyed the scene.

I hoped to find a gate of some kind, something we might force open to gain entry. I should have realised that the Martians had no need of such a weak point, as their tripods would simply step over the barrier. Through binoculars, the wall looked completely smooth, just as the panels fitted to the Ironclad were, and there would be no grip for a man to climb up. The plan was to set a charge at the base of one stake, detonate it from a safe distance, and then charge in before the Martians had time to react. We knew from our reconnaissance that there were no fighting machines inside the camp, and indeed no Martian activity at all. While we hoped that meant we might enter unopposed, only a fool would expect there to be no resistance.

"Stay at the rear, just as we planned," Webb reminded me in a whisper. He feared I would dive into battle, desperate to find and save my wife, and I can't say I blame him for his concern. After all, I was only here because I'd learned they had taken her prisoner. But now we were so close to the camp, I understood how out of my depth I was. I carried no weapon, and no idea how to use one. With no military training, and despite my time playing the war games, I had formed only a very basic understanding of the strategies and tactics that these men would need today. I would keep out of trouble, just as Amy would wish.

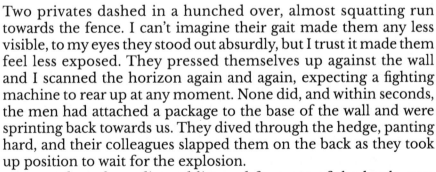

Two privates dashed in a hunched over, almost squatting run towards the fence. I can't imagine their gait made them any less visible, to my eyes they stood out absurdly, but I trust it made them feel less exposed. They pressed themselves up against the wall and I scanned the horizon again and again, expecting a fighting machine to rear up at any moment. None did, and within seconds, the men had attached a package to the base of the wall and were sprinting back towards us. They dived through the hedge, panting hard, and their colleagues slapped them on the back as they took up position to wait for the explosion.

I turned up the radio and listened for news of the battle over the hill from us. Russell kept barking orders at the rest of the soldiers, especially Lawrence in the Ironclad, but I heard very few responses from them. I suspect they were ignoring his back-seat commanding and just getting on with the matter at hand. From time to time the earth shook slightly beneath us as more of the Martian equipment exploded. Each one made my heart pause for an instant as I feared the Ironclad destroyed, but as long as I heard Russell bossing them around over the radio, I knew they were still fighting.

The tail end of a countdown brought my attention back to the camp before us.

"Three. Two. One." Webb intoned.

I put my fingers in my ears and ducked down slightly to avoid any possible shrapnel.

Silence.

I uncovered my ears and pushed myself back up to look at the camp again. As I did, a blinding white and yellow flash erupted, followed an instant later by a thump so deep it rattled my bones. Glints of metal flew above us, spearing trees and earth behind our position.

"Sorry Sergeant," one private said over the ringing in my ears. "Think the fuse was a little long."

"Go!" Webb shouted, everyone scrambled to their feet and charged at the new hole in the fence.

I struggled to keep up, weighed down with the radio. By the time I reached the still-smoking crater the explosives had created, the soldiers were already inside. They fanned out to cover the entrance, scanning in all directions for any Martian who might be inside. I saw none, Webb waved us all forward, and we started moving from building to building.

Each was constructed of a thin layer of the Martian metal, no thicker than a few sheets of paper but strong enough to resist the butt-end of a rifle slammed into it. A door was clearly outlined in the front of each, too small for a Martian to pass, but ideally sized for human occupants to come and go. An intricate mechanism sat mid way up one side, where a lock might be placed. One private was slamming his rifle into it, kicking it with his booted foot, and getting nowhere. I asked him to stop, bent down and examined the device. I felt the back of my neck tingling as I worked, and worked to put aside the thought that a Martian was peering at me. If one were present, the soldiers would take care of it.

Might they operate the lock remotely, I wondered. If so, we would need to find a control room or something similar, which would take time. No doubt they would have secured that building, and probably guarded it, too. Perhaps the Martians wouldn't waste complicated technology on us lowly humans, though, and this would be their equivalent of a bolt. It would stop the people inside from escaping, after all. Reluctantly, I slid my forefinger into the hole at the centre of the device and probed around. I expected it to feel warm, even moist. Perhaps the organic appearance of the device had led me to think it was alive. In fact, it was icy cold and metallic, but I found it no less unpleasant to poke about.

As my finger entered, the shape of the channel forced it upwards. Curling my finger as I went, I got it in to its full length, my palm facing upwards and my shoulder aching. The tip of my finger could move to the left or the right, to my left was a void, but to the right was a piece of metal. I pressed against it as hard as possible, but it would not move. So much for that idea.

"Fetch some ropes, and metal hooks," I called, and the soldiers dashed off to the trucks. The posts which formed the door frame were about as thick around as my wrist and echoed with a loud, low clang when struck. We wedged a hook in between one of them and the door, attached a rope, and strung the other end to one of the waiting trucks. The vehicle took up the strain, before pushing forward and hauling the rope tight, pulling against the post. At first nothing happened, the engine straining and wheels slipping in the soft earth. After a few moments, it became apparent that the top of the post had bent over slightly from vertical, and a cheer went up. The driver pushed the truck to full throttle, creeping forward and being pulled backward as if in a tug-of-war. The prisoners surged at the opening, tried to push through even the slightest gap, and I had visions of them being injured if the rope snapped.

"Get back," I shouted over the surging engine. "Move away!" No-one heeded my words. I could only pray that the rope would hold and do its job. Painfully slowly, the upright post leaned over, the gap between it and the wall growing by fractions of an inch. Hands pushed through, shoulders followed, and before long, children were being pushed up and over the mass of people and through the gap. The soldiers dashed to catch them as they fell, astonished at their lightness and fragility. Weeping and cries of joy drowned out the diesel engines as the prisoners got their first glimpse of safety.

With a final, protesting squeal, the bar bent sufficiently to allow the starving men and women within to escape. They pushed, fell over each other and trampled one another in their eagerness to leave, and we all set to work, pulling them free of the crush before they were injured. A few minutes was all it took to empty the camp, and we had around seventy souls added to our number.

We shared what food and water we had among them. They wolfed down every morsel, gulped the water as if they had crossed a desert.

"More, please, more," came the cry, and we gave them everything we could. With bellies at least partially filled, some signs of humanity returned to them, bewilderment and fear appearing on their faces in place of the pleading and hunger that had gone before. I took charge, ordering them to the trucks where the soldiers assisted them to climb in, or lifted them bodily where needed. The benches folded up against the sides, allowing more of the liberated to sit upon the floor, and we fit them all in the trucks without difficulty.

———————◄O►———————

No-one tried to leave the next cell when we pulled the door open, so I clambered through the opening to investigate. It was barely warmer inside the cell than outside, the only heat source being the bodies crammed into it. It smelt like nothing I had ever experienced before, and I recoiled instinctively and gagged. People lay on every inch of the floor, huddled together on the hard metal with only their dirty and ragged clothes to insulate them. Light came through a thin slit near the ceiling, barely enough to see by until I had opened the door. Grubby faces turned to me in terror and I realised my silhouette against the dazzling light from the doorway was probably not as reassuring as I might like.

"Come on," I urged them, "get out!"

The sound of distant gunfire and explosions spurred them into motion. Slowly, painfully, they hauled each other upright and stumbled towards the door. As they emerged blinking into the light, it revealed their emaciated bodies and sallow faces. How long had they been held here? Amy was not among them, something for which I was both grateful and concerned. She must be in one of the other buildings, I reasoned, and perhaps these were the longest-serving prisoners. She would not have had as long in captivity as these people.

Two figures at the rear of the room had not moved, and I stepped inside to rouse them. The smell overwhelmed me at once, and I found I could go no further. I felt a hand on my arm, stick thin and brittle, and turned to look into the sunken eyes of a man whose age was impossible to guess. He looked ancient, his face sunken and grime driven deep into every pore, but might have been younger than me. He shook his head and croaked a few words.

"They're gone," he said, with a nod at the figures. "Three days back." He shuffled away, barely able to put one foot in front of the other.

By now, the soldiers had opened almost every door, and people in varying states of health were issuing forth. Some were relatively clean and moved easily, while most were filthy and broken down by their ordeal. Not one of them spoke aloud.

I scanned every face for Amy, certain I would recognise my wife no matter how dirty or half-starved she might be, but there was no sign of her.

There was more gunfire over the horizon, and I turned up the radio to listen. What reports I could make out were garbled, the distance and the intervening hill muting or distorting the voices, but I gathered the Ironclad was on the run. So far, it had avoided damage, and I offered a silent prayer for Lawrence and his colleagues as I turned down the volume once more.

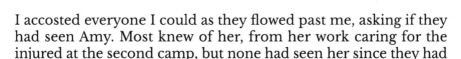

I accosted everyone I could as they flowed past me, asking if they had seen Amy. Most knew of her, from her work caring for the injured at the second camp, but none had seen her since they had arrived.

"Some people get taken," one man told me. "The doors open, a tentacle comes in, and they're gone." He shuddered.

"Where do they take them?" I asked, dread gnawing at me.

"How should we know," he replied with disdain, and joined the rest of the evacuating prisoners.

Had she truly gone? Was I too late to save her? I felt my nails digging into my palms as my fists clenched. If they had taken her from me, Russell would pay.

I dashed from cell to cell, peering inside each, my eyes straining to see a figure in the darkness. Finally, when I had all but given up hope, I saw someone. One petite figure was straining to support a larger one, neither recognisable in the gloom. As they moved towards the light, my heart sang.

"Amy!"

She almost dropped the man she was helping in surprise. "What the devil are you doing here?" she asked. "Never mind, give me a hand."

The man looked familiar, had he been in the protest at the camp gates? He might have been the one who confronted me, but in his emaciated state, I could not be sure. I supported his other arm over my shoulders, and together we got him out into the open. His left leg was crudely bandaged, his trousers cut open to allow access, and tendrils of vile green and purple infection peered out from beneath the dressings. He was clearly in agony, unable to put his foot to the ground, and I couldn't imagine he would survive long. I did not argue, however, and assisted him as best I could.

"I came to find you," I explained, grunting with the effort. "Russell didn't tell me, I only just found out, and then I couldn't stand by while..."

"Hush, now." I had expected anger, but she seemed genuinely pleased to see me. "You should have left it to the professionals, but I know that was never likely. You're a fool, but a brave one."

Most of the soldiers had gone ahead, guarding the first prisoners out and watching over the procession of escapees. A few had hung back to bring up the rear, Webb among them, and he urged us on. Abruptly his tone changed, the men snatched their rifles into firing position and took cover behind the cells.

"Get down!" Webb barked at us, and I risked a glance over my shoulder.

Behind us, not two hundred yards away, was a Martian.

Chapter Twenty-Four

Detonation

I t was riding one of the handling machines, a glass-like cupola atop a metal base, which moved about upon short legs. Three legs on each corner, in the manner of the fighting machines, spun and whirled in all directions as it moved closer. The effect was one of speed and stability; the creature perched in its glass dome not jolted or jostled. All this I saw in an instant.

Amy and I ducked behind one cell, hoping it had not seen us. The man we carried groaned in pain as his infected leg hit the ground, and I put my hand over his mouth to silence him. Without warning, I was back in the buried house; I heard the curate shouting and wailing beside me. I felt the heft of the meat chopper in my hand, the fear of discovery driving me to swing it... and then I felt Amy's hand upon mine, and I was back.

"Run!" a soldier called. Amy and I hoisted our burden off the cold ground and were about to dash for it when another voice called out, "hold fast!" We could not see the Martian or judge the danger for ourselves, and so we waited, muscles burning with the effort of holding the man upright, for the next instruction.

Soldiers rushed past our hiding spot towards the enemy, and they let rip a volley of gunfire towards the contraption. I was shaking so hard Amy felt it transmitted through the man propped between us.

"Put him down," she whispered. We lowered him carefully to the ground once more. Unable to stop my legs from crumbling beneath me, I fell into a heap next to him. In a flash, Amy was beside me, her arms tight around my body. I don't remember the next few moments clearly, but I know I cried out. They would overrun our hiding place, I was sure, and the Martian would take us.

"We must run!" I shouted, and Amy tried to silence me. "It's coming, we have to go!"

"Hush, please. Darling, you must be quiet," she whispered. I barely heard her over the shouts and screams of the soldiers, and the sound of the gunfire I was certain was in vain.

"Let us go," I told her, "leave this man here for the Martian, he can buy our freedom."

I will never forget the expression of despair on her face at my words. I can scarcely believe I considered such an idea, and even my abject terror can not excuse it.

Webb ducked behind the cell alongside us and grabbed me by the shirt-front. "Silence, man, for God's sake!" he hissed. But even this was not enough to still my voice.

"Get us to safety, won't you? Isn't that your job?"

He looked at me, at Amy, and at the man wide-eyed in terror beside us. With a curt nod, he dashed off once more. The last I saw of him was charging full speed towards the Martian, plucking a grenade from his belt.

A loud explosion suggested the grenade had found its target, and moments later we got the call to run once more.

Amy snapped instructions at me, ordering me to my feet, and I obeyed in a haze. When she told me to pick up the injured man once more, I didn't hesitate, but bent and dragged him to his feet. Together, we lifted him almost clear of the ground and set off as fast as possible towards safety.

I did not dare to glance back again, expecting at any moment to feel the cold metal grip of a tentacle tripping me. Ricochets and cracks from the bullets flying behind us sounded too close for comfort, and we half-dragged, half-carried our invalid towards the end of the row of cells.

Ahead of us the trucks were waiting, the last of the prisoners clambering or being lifted aboard. As we neared them, the first took off, leaving behind a cloud of dust and diesel smoke as it sped to safety. Our progress was slow enough that I didn't think there would be a vehicle waiting when we reached them, or even if we would. Like the worst nightmares that wake me in the early hours, the intervening distance seemed to grow and stretch before me. My legs were burning, my back spasming in protest by the time we finally closed the distance and handed our injured man up to the rear of the truck.

Now I looked back. They had held the Martian at bay, still too close for comfort but far enough as not to endanger the vehicles and our escape. Two of the soldiers lay dead, and as I watched, the whip-like motion of one of the handling tentacles sliced a third man almost in two. But then cracks formed in the transparent dome, the Martian recoiled, and scurried away. He must have feared contamination from our air, or perhaps that the next bullet might make it through and hit him. Either way, we were free.

—◆O◆—

Arms lifted us into the last of the trucks, and we made our way over the hill. Webb was nowhere to be seen, but the surviving soldiers crammed into the vehicle as before. I was about to ask about him when one of them spoke.

"The radio," he said, and grabbed the receiver from the pack on my back. How I had hauled that around and my share of the injured man, I do not know.

He called over the radio that we were clear, and we crested the rise.

The battlefield was strewn with the mangled remains of Martian machinery, each smoking away and some of them even still on fire. Our heat-ray had clearly been hard at work. I looked forward to hearing Lawrence's report on the battle, it must not have been easy to command that vehicle and strike so effectively at the heart of the enemy.

"Well done!" Chambers' voice came from the radio. "It was a close-run thing here, but we have them on the ropes."

The soldiers were cheering and congratulating each other when a loud bang and a puff of smoke emerged from the rear of the Ironclad. The vehicle's wheels and treads stopped instantly and the whole apparatus skidded to an abrupt halt. Absolute silence fell over us all.

"What happened?" I called over the radio, but no reply came. "Lawrence, are you there?"

After a few moments, the radio crackled into life. "Diesel engine... blew..." came Lawrence's voice, weak and pained. "Driver and gunner... dead."

"Can you get out of there?" I asked, fearing the reply I knew was coming.

"No, pinned under a beam," came the reply. "Listen..." A fit of coughing interrupted him. "Engine can't explode like that. Not possible. Someone..." More coughing. Ice gripped my heart. Sabotage?

"Are you suggesting...?" Russell asked. "No-one would dare!"

Lawrence sounded weaker yet, and I had to strain to hear him. "It was... some sort of timer, I think. Not one of the crew. Someone in... camp is fighting... against us."

The fighting machines were closing in slowly, tentative in case this was a trap. There was no way we could reach Lawrence before them, even assuming we might help him at all.

Amy must have had the same idea. "Keep going," she shouted to the driver. "We have to get the civilians to safety." The truck sped up.

"Can you reach the heat-ray? Or the guns?" I asked.

"No." Damn, if he'd been able to keep shooting, he might have stood a chance. "Look, Lawrence," I said. "Keep your head down and someone will come and get you. If the Martians see no movement, they might assume they stopped you and head out again."

"You know that won't happen," Russell snapped. "Now shut up, let me work." He spoke into the radio in a low, urgent tone. As our distance from the battle increased, we descended a hill, the radio lost signal and I could no longer make out what he was saying to Lawrence.

"Work? What the devil on?" I asked, ignoring the instruction. No reply came.

"What is he planning?" I asked Amy. "The engine's gone, Lawrence can't reach the heat-ray or the gun. And the reactor won't power the wheels..."

Mere moments later, the sky lit up behind us, and a glance over our shoulders showed a ball of fire rising slowly above the ridgeline. It was hard to assess the size of it, but we had little time to judge as a howling gale blew above our heads, whipping the trees around and uprooting the oldest and feeblest. The winds abruptly dropped, then reversed direction — blowing back towards the site of the blast, dragging soil and dust into our faces and forcing the truck to a halt.

---◄O►---

I called into the radio, hailing Lawrence, Chambers, Webb, even Russell. My desperation grew as no reply came from anyone. I checked and rechecked the radio, as far as I could tell it was operating normally, but perhaps the dust storm had found its way inside and upset the delicate workings.

The soldiers now looked to me for orders, and I confess I felt the panic rising once more. What could we do? Should we go back for the rest of our comrades? If any had even survived that explosion, they might well be prisoners of the Martians themselves by now. And if they had not...

"We press on," I decided. "As you said, the civilians are our priority."

The truck jerked into motion again, heading back to the camp. A half mile or so down the road, we came across another of the vehicles which had been struck by a blown-down tree. The front was caved in; the driver sitting by the side of the road with a bloodied head but miraculously alive. The former prisoners who had been aboard were milling around with no apparent purpose, still in a state of shock from their horrific treatment.

Amy leapt into action, checking on the injured driver and dressing his wound with a first-aid kit from the truck. I took a deep breath and ordered the soldiers to assess the civilians.

"Any who can walk will have to," I said. "Those who cannot, ride in the trucks. If there are any spaces left over, the women and children get them."

While we worked, a small group appeared on the road behind us. Blurred by the distance, it was impossible to make them out at first, and I assumed it would be people from nearby towns come to investigate the explosion. As they drew closer, I recognised a few of the soldiers who had stayed with the Ironclad, and then noticed that Russell and Chambers accompanied them.

"I thought you dead!" I called out. "What happened?"

Chambers merely shook his head. He looked pale, as if sick. Russell looked little better, but he at least explained.

"We blew up the reactor, in the Ironclad," he said, as if that explained anything.

"We did nothing, Lawrence did it," Chambers muttered under his breath.

"No matter," Russell said. "It felled the last of them, that's what matters."

The reactor. Icy dread filled me. "What about the radiation? Are we...?"

"You're safe," Russell said. "You were far enough away by then, and over the ridge. Any exposure would be minimal."

"But what about you?" I looked at Chamber's ghostly complexion again. I realised I had seen a similar pallor once before.

"We shall have to wait and see," Russell said, his eyes betraying his confident tone. "We were out of the direct line, so we ought to be alright."

———————◄O►———————

Amy wished to stay with me, but I would not hear of it. The sooner she reached safety, the happier I would be.

She argued, of course. "But I know more about the radiation sickness than anyone else here. I am best prepared to notice the warning signs, or help you if you are affected."

"And what help could you offer?" Russell replied. He winced under her glare. "I meant no slight upon your abilities. I only meant that without medical supplies, or a laboratory, you would be ill-equipped. You can best help the wounded in the vehicles."

"I must agree," I added. "And insist. I only came here to see you safe."

"Then come with me," she protested. "Another episode like..." she stopped, unwilling to tell the others of my brush with panic.

"I will be fine, Chambers and Russell will keep me busy enough," I joked.

Eventually, she accepted she would never change my mind. The trucks with their wounded set off at speed, a couple of soldiers perched on the running boards as a token defence, and Amy waving from the rear. The rest of us trudged along with our small military contingent towards the camp, unable to take solace in the victory. We had destroyed several Martian fighting machines, taken a base of operations out of action, and we could only hope that the invaders knew some fear at our having struck such a blow. But we knew we could not follow up the victory with another.

We had lost another reactor and the last of our Ironclads. The sacrifice of Lawrence hit us most strongly, and even Russell had the sense to hold his tongue. We were so lost in our thoughts that we didn't notice the Martian tripod standing among the trees until we were almost beneath it.

We scattered, diving for cover in the undergrowth even as we realised it could not have failed to have caught us. For an interminable minute we each lay there, trying to steady our breathing and waiting for the searing burn of the heat-ray —

but nothing came. I risked a look; raising my head and peering cautiously towards my foe.

It hadn't moved! Not stepped toward me, turned in my direction or even twitched one of the tentacles that hung from it. I looked closer, and noticed that they were just gently swaying in the wind, and not being driven with purpose as I had first believed. Russell also peeked out from his concealment, a look of puzzlement on his face.

We stood then, slowly approached the machine, poised at any moment to run or dive for cover, but no movement came. It might as well have been frozen in place. We spent some time examining it for damage, thinking some aspect of the blast had injured it even at this range of almost five miles, but we could not see even a scrape or scratch, nothing to explain its immobility.

We marked the position of the machine on our maps and continued on.

Chapter Twenty-Five

Reunion

As we climbed to higher ground, we glimpsed another fighting machine in the distance behind us, also immobile. By taking a bearing to it and estimating its distance from our location, we figured this one stood around four miles from the refuelling station.

"That cannot be coincidence," Russell said. "Something in the blast has upset them, destroyed their workings or otherwise rendered them inert."

"And the radio too?" I asked. "What effect might it have on us?" Visions of a slow, painful death in crisp white hospital sheets assaulted me, and I fought down panic.

"The pain comes on quickly," he replied, his words not as reassuring as he intended. "We're still moving, let's not assume the worst."

It took an age to reach the camp, and I spent every step wondering if my tiredness was merely a reaction to the day's events or a symptom of my impending doom. Russell also slowed, stumbling from time to time over roots and upturned rocks, and we rejoiced when the camp hove into view shortly before sundown.

People helped us inside, and pressed food and water into our hands. I hadn't realised how hungry and thirsty I had been — we had freely donated our rations to those who needed them more — and I felt my energy flooding back as I ate and drank. The truck had arrived a few hours before, and set out to find and retrieve us, but clearly missed us somehow. Its occupants were being tended to in the infirmary and the doctors expected almost all to recover. Everyone pressed around us, eager to learn more of the story, and I retreated into my thoughts. I barely heard Russell giving a broad outline of the facts before I slipped into sleep.

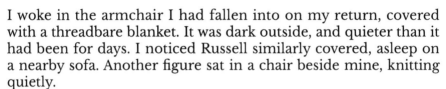

I woke in the armchair I had fallen into on my return, covered
with a threadbare blanket. It was dark outside, and quieter than it
had been for days. I noticed Russell similarly covered, asleep on
a nearby sofa. Another figure sat in a chair beside mine, knitting
quietly.

"Amy," I croaked, my mouth dry.

"Oh, thank the Lord!" she said when she saw me awake. "They
told me you were unhurt, that you were just exhausted, but you
slept so deeply..." and even in the gloom, I could see tears run down
her cheeks.

"The Ironclad, the reactor," I started the sentence a few times, but
halted when she began nodding.

"Everyone is fine," she said. "The blast was small, and the hill
sheltered us well enough from it. They expect some radiation in
the area for some time, which might well hold the Martians back
from investigating. But it seems we had a lucky escape."

"Chambers, Russell too?" I nodded in his direction.

"The doctors took blood from everyone," she said, gesturing to a
small bandage at my elbow I hadn't noticed. "Stained the samples
to check leukocyte levels. We understood from my former patient
what to look for, what the early signs were, and there's no cause for
concern. I admit I didn't understand it all but from that other poor
fellow's example, they said you would be fine." I slumped back in
my chair, relief flooding me. The blast hadn't condemned me.

I took my wife's hand, grasped her fingers, and we sat there
together in the dark until we fell asleep.

Sun streaming through the windows woke me, my neck sore from
a night in a thinly padded armchair. Amy and Russell had left, no
doubt back to their duties. Russell could wait, so I set off to the
infirmary, where I was sure I would find Amy hard at work.

Almost every bed was occupied now, but as the more emaciated
of the former prisoners required little more than supervision
and rehydration, pillows propped up the majority and they were
reading or talking among themselves. The skeleton staff of the
infirmary were rushed off their feet, however, by the walking

wounded. Most of the ailments were minor injuries, but without treatment in the squalid conditions of the Martian prison, several them were badly infected. I knew from bitter experience how unlikely they would be to recover. Among them I spotted the man Amy and I had carried to safety, leaning on a crutch, his colour much improved. His leg still bore a bandage, but the discoloured tendrils of infection were no longer visible beyond the edges of the fabric.

"Remarkable, isn't it?" Amy said beside me. I turned and embraced her.

"How...?" I started.

"Some new drugs they were working on at the other site before it fell. Fights against bacteria like nothing else we've used before."

"I'm surprised Russell let you take it," I said. "Or even told you it existed."

"Well, he wasn't around to ask," she smiled. "And it wasn't hard to figure out he was doing something unusual when my patients over there got better without my help. I sent the couriers out last night once we got back. They're fetching as much as they can carry, running in relays. Just as well too, we're using it as fast as they can bring it in."

"He won't be happy," I warned her. "But I doubt that would stop you. How did they even discover such a miracle?"

"Through examination of the Martian technology and equipment. We suspected they had some means to combat bacteria, so the biologists went looking."

"That's not all they were looking for," I said. "Russell confirmed they were hoping for a germ that could breach their defences, to use against them."

"If it led to this drug, I'm not going to complain." She bent closer to my ear and whispered. "We'd have lost at least twenty by now without it, so I don't much care if he made a deal with the Devil himself."

"You're fine with him having that power?"

"No, I'd much rather it was in better hands. But how else are we to win this war? Even the Ironclads and flying machine, as remarkable as they were, barely made a scratch when you consider the wider picture, and at what cost? Bacteria worked for us last time, so we shouldn't shy away from recruiting them again."

She wasn't wrong, of course, but was my squeamishness only because of my doubt about Russell's motives?

"Now, there's someone here who will want to speak to you," Amy said with a slight grin. Sergeant Webb lay in one of the beds, a bandage around his head but a smile on his face.

"You made it?" I gasped. "I thought for sure..."

"For a moment I wasn't certain myself," he replied. "But I'm glad you're both safe."

I couldn't find the words to thank him. He had thrown himself into danger to protect us, while I cowered and shook. I felt tears pricking at my eyes, and when Webb simply nodded to say he understood, I was forced to turn away.

***

I found Russell and Chambers in the camp's map room, a bustle of activity surrounding him, and the table upon which many of the wooden tripod figures gathered. A chalk circle occupied a portion of the map, and all the figures inside this lay flat rather than standing upright. Chambers spotted me and called me over.

"It's about a six-mile radius," he said, words falling over each other in his excitement. "Everything electrical inside that has failed — including the Martian machines! That's what happened to our radio. Reports have been coming in overnight and this morning, as the radio operators realise their equipment is dead they're sending runners to us — from that and the few reports we've had in from those with working gear, we've sketched out the effect of that blast."

"I'm glad you're feeling better. So if a reactor goes up, they stop?" I said, struggling to follow his rapid-fire explanation.

"Exactly! We're already making plans to rig up small versions of the Ironclads with that remote operation equipment, drive them into position and detonate. We should be able to create corridors clear of the damned Martians and regroup safely."

"Can we even build them?" I asked. "We haven't any factories, just a few anvils and smelters."

Chambers shook his head. "Not full sized, no. But we don't need them to be. They can be made just strong enough to carry a small reactor. We could use trucks if need be, but the Ironclad design can handle rougher terrain."

"You also said that remote control equipment wouldn't work, it was hard to control," I pointed out.

"We don't need to be precise, with an area of effect that large!"

He had an answer for everything. "But if we can't go within miles without our gear failing, what good is that?" I asked.

"It's only at the moment of the blast," he explained. "After that, it's safe to traverse again. The soldiers are already inspecting the wreckage and recovering their dead, and our radio operators found that their spares kits are not affected. Only powered-up equipment dies, your radio was in use when Lawrence..." he tapered off, his excitement waning as he remembered. "They didn't die in vain," he continued more calmly. "But we can't keep scavenging reactors from fallen machines. We need to build our own, if they just need to go bang, they should be within our capability."

"Build them? From what, exactly? They don't run on coal, after all."

Russell spoke now for the first time. "Before the invasion, we had men working on it," he informed me. "I couldn't tell you before, it was top secret. They have some ideas — a chemical element found in pitchblende looks the most promising, and it is probably what the Martians themselves use."

"I thought you were pinning our hopes on the biological front?" I asked.

Chambers looked between us in confusion, and Russell gave me a glare. Evidently, I was the only one who had discovered his secret so far.

"Well, yes, it's the most promising line of research, or was until this happened. But what's wrong with having a backup plan?"

As glad as I was to see Chambers and Russell in temporary agreement, something still nagged at me. "Pitchblende? We don't have any of that in England," I protested. "Where are you proposing to find it?"

"Are you interested in taking a trip to Canada?" Russell asked.

THE STORY CONTINUES IN

EARTH UNDER THE MARTIANS

COMING SOON

Notes

This is a work of fiction. However, where possible I have chosen to ground it in reality as closely as I can. In addition I have included references to other of Well's writings, and these notes will illustrate some connections that may be of interest to the reader.

Chapter 1 - Woking

Mars moved into opposition
'Opposition' is an astronomical term, meaning Mars is on the opposite side of the Earth from the Sun. This is when the two planets are closest together, and was the opportunity taken by the Martians in the original novel to invade.
https://ares.watch/opposition

Two years had passed since the terrible events of the Martian invasion
Wells' original novel is undated, but some clues place it in around 1907. This sequel takes place in 1909, although following Wells' example I have not made this explicit.
I agree with the deductions made by Kenneth Hite at https://ares.watch/dates

Amy asked
The original novel named none of the characters beyond Ogilvy the astronomer. The narrator in the original met so few people that it was fine to refer to them by occupation, but I have broken from this tradition for ease of reading.
Amy is the name chosen by the creators of the BBC dramatisation, and I have elected to use that name here. She was almost named Carrie after the character in Jeff Wayne's musical version.
https://ares.watch/bbc
https://ares.watch/musical

The machine that once towered over Primrose Hill
This was left as a monument at the end of the original novel — children played around its legs.

the Martian kept preserved under spirits in the Natural History Museum
Also mentioned at the end of the original novel.

why not visit Frederick in London
Frederick was the brother's name in the BBC adaptation, and I have adopted it here.

the saloon bar of the Spotted Dog
The local pub of the narrator.

Doubtless the initial explosions at research laboratories in the capital
South Kensington and Ealing laboratories are mentioned in the original novel.

The Indian rebellion and the war in Crimea
Both real-life events from around the time Wells was writing.
https://ares.watch/rebellion
https://ares.watch/crimea

Another, global conflict to come
Obviously referring to the First World War in our history, probably never to occur in this timeline given the events of the rest of this book.

———————◄O►———————

Chapter 2 - Brother

I strolled along to Whitehall
The seat of government in the UK. Most of the buildings are occupied by various government departments.

I sauntered over to Hyde Park
One of London's glorious open green spaces.

https://ares.watch/hyde

A jeering crowd over at Speaker's Corner
A region of Hyde Park where speakers can talk on any subject.
https://ares.watch/speaker

astronomical observations by Lessing
Mentioned in the original, as a reason for hope that the Martians might be trying that planet instead.

Some of our citizens were temporary refugees in the nearer regions of the Continent
Many reached France before the fall of the Martians, and returned almost as soon as was possible.

At the gathering in August Mr Watt-Evans cornered me
Apologies to Lawrence Watt-Evans, whose contribution to 'The War of the Worlds: Fresh Perspectives on the H.G. Wells Classic [ISBN:978-19321005-6]' I have abused here. I recommend the book and Watt-Evans' article in particular.
https://ares.watch/perspectives

canals dug to bring what little water remained to the vast cities
Wells wrote at a time when the 'Canals on Mars' theories were in full effect. We now know that they were optical illusions, not vast waterways.
https://ares.watch/canal

Martian equivalent of the Chartists
Chartism was a movement in the UK in the mid-1800s, pushing for social reform. While describing themselves as non-violent, some supporters in Newport in 1839 did inspire riots and were transported as punishment.
https://ares.watch/chartist

Chapter 3 - Chambers

we have reason to believe it can be transferred by radio

Experimental forms of television existed in the 1920s, I have assumed that the Martians' arrival accelerated the invention.

controlled decomposition of certain minerals
Nuclear understanding was in its infancy in the period, but it's not a huge stretch to imagine the Martians had adopted it.

research of Becquerel, Rutherford and others
Henri Becquerel was a French scientist, and the first to discover the phenomenon of radioactivity. He shared the Nobel prize with Marie and Pierre Curie. Marie Curie coined the term 'radioactivity' as a result of her work on Radium.
Ernest Rutherford was a New-Zealand born scientist who has been described as the father of nuclear physics.

Scattered over the map were miniature figures of men
Obviously a regular feature of military planning, table-top or miniature wargaming is also discussed in H.G. Wells' book Little Wars.
The full (and rather sexist) title was "*Little Wars: a game for boys from twelve years of age to one hundred and fifty and for that more intelligent sort of girl who likes boys' games and books*"
https://ares.watch/little

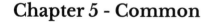

Chapter 4 - Panic

church bells were silenced
Church bell ringing was banned in 1940 as the bells would be reserved to signal a German invasion, but this ban was lifted in 1943 when the danger of invasion was felt to have reduced.
https://ares.watch/bells

Chapter 5 - Common

the sand unable to drain after our wet summer
1909 was a particularly cool, wet and cloudy year.

my short tenure as a teacher
Wells worked as a teacher for a short while, so I have assumed the Narrator also did.

The coming of the day of God
2 Peter 3:12-13 (quoted from the King James Version). In the New International Version it reads:

> *as you look forward to the day of God and speed its coming. That day will bring about the destruction of the heavens by fire, and the elements will melt in the heat. But in keeping with his promise we are looking forward to a new heaven and a new earth, where righteousness dwells.*

Therefore hath the curse devoured the earth
Isiah 24:6 (quoted from the King James Version). In the New International Version it reads:

> *Therefore a curse consumes the earth; its people must bear their guilt. Therefore earth's inhabitants are burned up, and very few are left.*

How far could we cycle in a day
Wells was a great advocate of cycling, which went through a craze around the start of the 20th Century before the advent of the automobile. He wrote a comic novel in the vein of 'Three Men in a Boat' about it, called 'The Wheels of Chance: A Bicycling Idyll'.
https://ares.watch/cycle

The Necropolis
Brookwood Cemetery or the London Necropolis was designed to replace all of London's burial grounds as the capital grew. As the city expanded old cemeteries were often dug up and the

bodies transferred to Brookwood. The site was served by a special railway (The Necropolis Railway) which had facilities to handle first-, second- and third-class passengers, and coffins similarly segregated. Coffin tickets were of course one-way.

https://ares.watch/brookwood

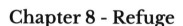

Chapter 8 - Refuge

Land Ironclad
The idea of tanks was in the air around the end of the 19th Century, and Wells himself had an idea for these which he detailed in a short story of the same name. He denied 'inventing' the tank, saying that when he saw the tanks used in WW1 they were not at all what he had in mind. "Yet let me state at once that I was not their prime originator. I took up an idea, manipulated it slightly, and handed it on." His used 'pedrail wheels' instead of caterpillar tracks, being wheels with feet mounted to them.

https://ares.watch/ironclad

Chapter 9 - Setback

how it kills so quickly, and needing such tiny quantities to do so
This is reminiscent of some nerve agents, which were unknown in Wells' time. However his descriptions of the black smoke were horribly prescient of the use of gas in the trenches of World War 1 shortly after the book was published.

perhaps an anti-bacterial drug of some sort
This is well before the discovery of Penicillin, in 1928.

Chapter 10 - Sighting

a quarry somewhere in Wiltshire
This is a reference to CGWHQ (Central Government War Headquarters, codenamed BURLINGTON), under MoD Corsham in Wiltshire. A former quarry, repurposed during WW2 as an underground engine factory, it was designated in 1955 as the seat of government in the event of a nuclear war. During the time period of this novel it would have been a working quarry.
https://ares.watch/wiltshire

A Tommy Stove
A small, solid fuel stove that was terribly inefficient. Used in WW1 and refined as time went on.
https://ares.watch/tommy

Bully beef
The name for corned beef (salted, cured beef in a tin) at the time.
https://ares.watch/bully

Brewed with the heat of the Ironclad's engine
Yes, British tanks really do have a tea kettle built in, although it's electrical in modern fighting vehicles. (And so do American tanks, since both use it for heating food rations without leaving the safety of the vehicle).
https://ares.watch/tea

William Kite
I trust my friend and ardent supporter will forgive me for borrowing his name for the Ironclad.
https://ares.watch/kite

Heliograph
A signalling mirror that reflects the light of the sun.
https://ares.watch/heliograph

Chapter 13 - Massacre

His skin beneath the burns looked pallid
For more detail on the terrifying effects of excessive exposure to radiation, see the long history of nuclear accidents and in particular Louis Slotin's death.
https://ares.watch/radiation

Chapter 14 - Flight

There were small teams of men, saboteurs or guerrilla fighters
I based this idea on the Auxiliary Units, members of the Home Guard in WW2 who would have gone to ground in the event of a Nazi invasion.
https://ares.watch/aux
https://ares.watch/guard

strapped small, powerful steam engines to their aircraft
A reference to the Wright Brothers. Part of their first flyer (which was, in fact, steam powered) has now flown on Mars attached to the Ingenuity helicopter.
https://ares.watch/wright

"How does that work?" — "Very well,"
Much Science Fiction bends the rules of science for dramatic effect, and this book is no exception. Star Trek is notorious for it, including 'Heisenberg Compensators' in the transporter equipment to get around the uncertainty principle which would render such a device practically and indeed theoretically impossible. When asked by Time magazine in 1994, "How do the Heisenberg compensators work?" Michael Okuda replied, "They work just fine, thank you."
https://ares.watch/compensate

produce a gravity insulating effect
This is not the same method as Cavorite, used in Wells' "The First Men in the Moon", but the effect is similar.
https://ares.watch/cavorite

Chapter 17 - Exodus

directly into the line of claymores here
Claymores are a directional mine, used against personnel. While they were only invented in the 1960s, I have taken the liberty of assuming they might be developed earlier to attack the legs of a walking machine.
https://ares.watch/claymore

Chapter 18 - Retribution

exotic succulents I have seen at Kew
Kew Gardens has been the home of the Royal Botanical Society since 1840, but has existed far longer as a reservoir of botanical life. These days it also includes a seed bank of endangered species.
https://ares.watch/kew

Chapter 24 - Detonation

Taking some liberties — the blast is modelled on this:
https://ares.watch/blast
I have assumed that with the men behind a rise they would escape the initial radiation burst even though that should extend about half a mile. The same topography would shield them from the worst of the blast, and if they were more than about six hundred yards away they would probably survive that even without protection.

Chapter 25 - Reunion

stained the samples to check leukocyte levels
White blood cells were discovered in the 1870s, and while haematology was in its infancy during this time period, a simple microscope would allow this level of analysis.
https://ares.watch/whitebloodcell

Fights against bacteria like nothing else
While penicillin (the first antibiotic) was not discovered until 1928, reverse engineering something similar from a pre-existing discovery is not too far-fetched an idea.
https://ares.watch/penicillin

So if a reactor goes up, they stop
Electro-Magnetic Pulse (EMP) is a feature of nuclear explosions, but I've slightly exaggerated its effects here. Radios of the time period would probably not be affected, but again I've assumed some accelerated progress as as result of the Martian technology being available.
https://ares.watch/emp

chemical element found in pitchblende
Pitchblende is the older name for uraninite, a uranium ore. Marie Curie used this as the raw materials for her own researches at about this time.
https://ares.watch/pitchblende

Can you help me out?

T hank you so much for reading this book, and I'd love to know what you thought of it.

Reviews are vital for an author, not just so we can find out what people think, but because it also helps more readers like you find the books they're going to love. So please do consider leaving a review on Amazon.

If you're not sure how, it's very simple:

Click here to leave a review!

Get your free book!

V isit my website to claim your free book, "Amy's Journal".

https://ares.watch/amy

During the first Martian invasion, we all know what happened to our narrator. But after he left his wife in the care of her cousin in Leatherhead, what happened to her?

Abandoned by her husband amidst the terror of the Martian Invasion, Amy battles to help those in need and save lives. But when the war arrives on her doorstep, can she save herself?

Also By Mark Hood

War of the Worlds Sequels

Amy's Journal (website exclusive)

The Return of the Martians
Earth Under the Martians - Coming soon!

Fae Defence Society Series

Jacob's War
The Fairies Want Me Dead - Coming soon!

Tales from the Treehouse Anthologies

A is for Apple - contains my short story Skin Deep

B is for Beauty - contains my short story West of the Moon

Acknowledgments

I'd like to thank my beta readers for ploughing through the rough drafts of this book, and offering such great feedback. Joe, Kell, Darren: it's stronger and better because of you.

My super-supportive critique group, author circle, whatever we call ourselves – your support and encouragement was vital to the completion of this story, as was your criticism and butt-kicking. It literally couldn't have existed without you. Adam, Darren, Jan, Lynne, Tara: thank you.

The Bestseller Experiment Academy and Facebook Group, a source of wonder, challenge and support like nothing else I've found online.

Martyne, for being a rock and a sounding board – this is for you.

Anyone I've inevitably forgotten, or whose tiny interactions kept me motivated. Thank you.

And thanks to you too, reader, for taking a chance on this book.

About the Author

Mark Hood is an author living and working in the English county of Shropshire which allows him plenty of opportunities to stare out of the window at gorgeous scenery when he ought to be writing.

A life-long fan of science-fiction, classic and modern, he has long been an admirer of H. G. Well's writing. This series of unofficial sequels were sparked by wondering what we might learn from the Martian technology, and how that might allow us to prepare for the invader's return.

He also brings a life-long fascination with mythical creatures and ancient legends to his fantasy writing, which merges folklore and myth with the real world.

Find out more at https://markhoodauthor.com/ or reach out on Twitter @markhood

Milton Keynes UK
Ingram Content Group UK Ltd.
UKHW021015290724
446271UK00014B/674

9 781913 442163